CHECKMATE
IN THE
CARPATHIANS

PASSPORT TO DANGER

◆

The Secret of the Mezuzah

The Sagebrush Rebellion

Checkmate in the Carpathians

PASSPORT TO DANGER • BOOK THREE

CHECKMATE
IN THE
CARPATHIANS

M A R Y
R E E V E S
B E L L

BETHANY HOUSE PUBLISHERS
MINNEAPOLIS, MINNESOTA 55438

YA
BEL

Checkmate in the Carpathians
Copyright © 2000
Mary Reeves Bell

Cover illustration by Cheri Bladholm
Cover by Lookout Design Group, Inc.

Published by Bethany House Publishers
A Ministry of Bethany Fellowship International
11400 Hampshire Avenue South
Minneapolis, Minnesota 55438
www.bethanyhouse.com

Printed in the United States of America by
Bethany Press International, Minneapolis, Minnesota 55438

The Library of Congress has Cataloging-in-Publication Data

Bell, Mary Reeves, 1946
    Checkmate in the Carpathians / by Mary Reeves Bell.
      p. cm. — (Passport to danger ; bk. 3)
    Summary: A skiing trip to Romania with the new American ambassador becomes more exciting than they had planned when Constantine Kaye and his friend Hannah visit the estate of Con's elderly neighbor and become involved in a rally of neo-Nazis in Romania.
    ISBN 1-55661-551-5
    [1. Antisemitism—Fiction. 2. Prejudices—Fiction. 3. Jews—Romania—Fiction. 4. Romania—Fiction.] I. Title.
PZ7.B41166 CH   2000
[Fic]—dc21   99-051013

5,99

For my sons

Robert and Wesley

Special thanks to the real heroes, Matthew Hanrahan in Iasi and the staff of Romanian Christian Enterprises in Arad, for bringing creative assistance and God's love to the "least of these" His children. And to my friend Mariana Fasie for research assistance in Romania.

MARY REEVES BELL grew up on a cattle ranch in Wyoming. As an adult, she spent several years in Austria, where she studied Hebrew and Holocaust literature at the University of Vienna. Mary frequently travels to Romania, where she works with abandoned children. She and her husband, David, have three sons and four granchildren and currently live in Virginia.

CONTENTS

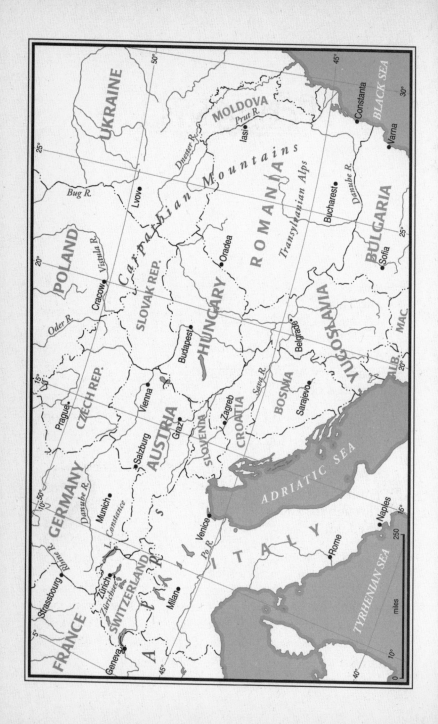

PROLOGUE

HANS GRUNWALD WAS FURIOUS. HIS ICY BLUE EYES STARED straight ahead as he struggled against an urge to smash something. Preferably his boss. Or the miniature plastic Christmas tree still stuck on the table a week after the holiday was history. Grunwald felt no Christmas spirit, belated or otherwise, and the pathetic tree only added to his rotten mood.

Despite being bundled up in heavy coats, neck scarves, and leather gloves, the two men seated at the table in front of him still shivered in the cold room. But Grunwald was hot with anger. "What do you mean you have a job for me in *Romania*?" he stormed.

Grunwald knew he was on thin ice with his boss. Knut Brofman commanded fear and respect from all members of the Odessa, and in his rage, Grunwald was dangerously close to going too far in questioning Brofman's orders.

"I refuse to go to that lousy country, especially all the way up to Iasi," he thundered.

The older man remained silent.

Grunwald was still a follower of the neo-Nazi ideals of the Odessa, which wanted to restore Germany and the Aryan race to their former glory under Hitler. But he didn't like the assignment Brofman was giving him, and he didn't much like his superior or taking orders from him, either.

Grunwald and Brofman had worked together last year on an assignment in Vienna; it had not gone well. First, they failed to kill their target, Nazi-hunter Simon Wiesenthal. Then they were arrested in Zürich while trying to withdraw Odessa money from a Swiss bank. The problems only increased the tension between them, as each blamed the other for the failures that had eventually landed them both in prison.

But most of all, Grunwald blamed the American brat who had actually outsmarted *him*—a well-trained professional terrorist. He was determined that the boy would pay for his year of misery in that stinking Swiss prison. From the moment a month ago when he was liberated by his Odessa comrades while being transported to a maximum-security prison, Grunwald had only one goal: to find and get rid of Constantine Kaye.

Grunwald knew it had been dangerous even to go near the boy, what with warrants for his arrest posted on every border crossing and police station in half a dozen countries. So he had been careful as he stalked his prey. Careful and successful.

Getting the boy's address, number 49A Braungasse in the Seventeenth District of Vienna, had been the tricky part. But once he found the corrupt Viennese policeman ready to sell that information, it was just a matter of price—settled over a pint of beer in a smoky Bierhaus.

The rest had been easy. Grunwald marveled at the Kayes' neighbors' willingness to talk about the American family living on Braungasse. Everyone remembered the excitement last year that had disturbed their usually quiet neighborhood on the edge of the Vienna Woods. The people eagerly whispered to him tales of an old man—a Nazi war criminal on the run—who supposedly had kidnapped a Jewish friend of the Kayes right there on Braungasse. But most revealing were the stories of Mrs. Kaye spying for the Nazi-hunter Simon Wiesenthal.

Though none of the neighbors admitted as much, it was clear to Grunwald that most of them wished the old Jewish troublemaker had been silenced. And they did say that foreigners who interfered in other people's history were no longer welcome on Braungasse.

Grunwald, who knew how to hunt for people himself, had listened carefully to all of the gossip and stories on the street. He discovered that his young nemesis, Con, and his widowed mother had lived alone in the big apartment until she married Nigel Kaye, a wealthy British businessman, two years ago. Con had only recently taken Kaye as his last name. Grunwald also learned that Con and his mother had been in Austria since he was a baby, so despite his American passport, the boy spoke flawless German. This explained a lot about their encounter in Zürich. It made Grunwald crazy with rage to think about it.

And now—with his plan for revenge ready to be carried out—the Odessa was ordering Grunwald to Romania, to some forgotten, run-down city on the other side of nowhere in eastern Europe.

"This is craziness," Grunwald yelled, bringing his thoughts back to Brofman. "Iasi is nearly in the Ukraine. It could take days just to get across the Carpathian Mountains. If the snow sets in I could be stranded there for weeks. No way. I'm not going. Not till I've taken care of that smart-mouth kid who put us both in prison."

Brofman remained silent, and Grunwald felt his temper build. A truck rumbled by on the A-16 Autobahn, heading west toward Vienna and rumbling the windowpane in its wake. This tiny village of Zemendorf, Austria—a checkpoint on the Hungarian border—was no better than Iasi, and Grunwald was eager to return to Vienna and exact his revenge.

When Brofman finally spoke, it was in a gravelly voice filled with sarcasm and authority. "Refuse? You refuse to carry out an order of the Odessa?" He drew out the double *s*, making it sound like a hiss. "You dare to refuse an order from your superior when so recently your Kameraden spent a vast amount of money and risked their lives to get you out of prison? Remember that oath of loyalty you swore to the Odessa?" Brofman was standing now, his anger erupting in waves as he hammered away at Grunwald. "Refuse the Odessa? I don't think so."

Grunwald held up his hands, as if to deflect the tirade, aware that he had gone too far. "I didn't mean refuse . . . exactly," he tried to explain. "I was upset. Of course I'm still one of the Kameraden. It's . . . it's just the timing. Give me a week, just one week. Then I'll go to Iasi. I'll go anywhere you ask."

Another truck rumbled by. The older man sat back down, his face a mask Grunwald was unable to read. After a few tense moments of silence, he began to hope his superior had changed his mind. But when Brofman spoke, his words dropped like little exploding bombs into the already disturbed brain of Hans Grunwald.

"You *will go* where I say . . . and *you will go tonight*. And try," he said sarcastically, "not to make any more mistakes like you did in Zürich. Kidnapping those"—Knut was enjoying mocking the angry man—"*children* who managed to outsmart a trained soldier like you."

"Enough!" Grunwald yelled. "I will make up for any mistakes I might have made in the past. And let me remind *you* of all the successful jobs I did before that rotten kid spotted me. Let me take care of him, and I will be more than ready to serve the cause—"

"This job will not wait," Brofman interrupted. "Your personal problem *will have to!*"

The discussion was over; an ultimatum had been given. Brofman laid a thick manila envelope on the rickety table.

"Tonight you go to Iasi and do as you are told, or we will

see to it that the Austrian police find *you* long before you find Constantine Kaye."

Grunwald knew he was defeated. He picked up the bulging envelope marked only with the death's-head insignia in the upper left-hand corner. His hands trembled, and the cold of that miserable room began to sink into his bones. He listened to his instructions without meeting the other man's eyes.

"Inside you will find the name of your contact in Iasi, a false passport, and your first-class train ticket on the Bucharest Express, which you will pick up at two-thirty tonight in Oradea. Wolfgang here, who has contacts with the Hungarian and Romanian police, will get you over this border at Zemendorf, across Hungary, and onto the train at Oradea. Thanks to Interpol, your face is all over the Internet and on posters at border crossings from here to Moscow, so you will need Wolfgang's contacts to get on the train. But the rest is up to you. And by the way, 'Dirty Harry,' " Brofman sneered, "don't get distracted by some little kids and mess this one up, too."

Loud guffaws broke out from both men at the reminder of what Grunwald's young accuser had called him on the witness stand.

The taunt worked; Grunwald's fist flew. The cheap Christmas tree smashed against the wall, its fake branches flying in all directions. He tucked the envelope under his arm and stormed out—heading for Romania in a very bad mood.

13

THE TRAIN

ANDREW HART MISSED THE TRAIN. NOT BY MUCH. BUT HE missed it all the same.

Hannah hung out of the train window, laughing into the wind as the old diesel engine picked up speed and left the hapless guy collapsed beside the track.

"Stop laughing and shut the window," I shouted over the noise at my wacky friend. "It's freezing in here!"

I pulled her back inside and struggled to shove the rusty window closed. It took both of us, but finally the lock clicked into position, shutting out the wind and cold and drifting snow. We dropped onto either side of the bright red high-back seats in the first-class coach of the Bucharest Express, laughing at our luck.

"Romania, here we come!" I roared. "Without our chaperone!"

Hannah's skin was pink from the cold wind and excitement. Her black hair had blown into a curly halo around her smiling face.

"Did you see poor Andrew Hart run?" I said gleefully, rubbing my hands together to start the blood flowing again.

"It's not funny, Con," Hannah said, still laughing. "Not funny at all." She slapped my upturned palms, trying to stop the giggles, which were rare for her. Hannah was usually not a giggler. In fact, she had very few of the annoying habits known to most girls. Which is why she was my best friend—had been ever since Mom and I moved to Vienna two years ago.

Hannah was wearing a dark blue ski jacket over a hooded sweat shirt, jeans tucked into wool socks, and hiking boots—looking ready for our train ride over the Carpathian Mountains. And we had just left Andrew Hart—the guy sent to accompany us—eating diesel fumes and dreading the wrath of his boss, Hannah's uncle, the Very Honorable Aaron Goldberg, recently appointed American ambassador to Romania.

"Not funny at all for him," she went on laughing, stomping her feet on the metal floor. "But you must admit this is *some* way to start our holiday!"

I couldn't have agreed more.

It had been only one hour ago, 11:00 P.M. exactly, when Hannah and I arrived at the Budapest, Hungary, train terminal. Even though we had plenty of time to find our train and make the midnight departure to Romania, we went to our connecting track straightaway—as we had been instructed over and over ad nauseam by our parents when they put us on the train in Vienna.

Stopping only to buy some roasted sausages and chestnuts from an old woman cooking over hot coals in a rusty barrel, we found track number 1 without any trouble. The annoying sound of badly played Christmas music—one week after the holiday was over—boomed from a loudspeaker into the mostly empty terminal.

Surprised—but not disappointed—to find our train car still empty, we proceeded to settle in, complaining all the while about the man who had been assigned to accompany us. Mr. Andrew Hart of the American embassy in Romania had been sent by Hannah's uncle to meet us in Budapest and escort us on our trip. We washed our spicy sausages and hot chestnuts down with Coke, protesting the insult while we awaited the arrival of Mr. Hart.

Only, he didn't arrive. At five minutes to twelve, with still no sign of him, we dropped the window, leaned out, and looked up the track, wondering nervously what to do. Which would upset our parents more—if we went on without him, or if we got off and were stranded overnight in the Budapest terminal? As the whistle blew and the train took its first jerk forward—too late for us to get off or anyone else to get on—a well-dressed young man, trench coat flying, came running madly down track number 1, trying to leap onto the departing train.

"It's him," Hannah had shouted, waving her scarf out the window. "Yahoo, Mr. Hart! Run!"

And run he did. The look of despair on his face made us sorry—almost—that he missed the train. Midtwenties-ish, with short brown hair and a starched, button-down preppy look, he looked fit. But his sprint was not enough. He grasped desperately at the last door on the last car of the Bucharest Express, then slid exhausted to his knees.

We waved as he became only a spot on the cement track leading back into the old terminal. A man in big trouble with his new boss. We were joining Hannah's uncle Aaron and aunt Ruth for a skiing holiday in the Carpathian Mountains. Escorting us there was probably Mr. Hart's first assignment for the new ambassador, and I didn't think his career in the Foreign Service was looking too hot at the moment.

"I hope Andrew Hart has a good excuse for missing the train," I said to Hannah, finally beginning to warm up. "Like the cab driver had a heart attack on the way to the station . . . or traffic was backed up by Russian tanks invading Budapest again . . . or marauding Mongol hoards . . . or . . ."

Hannah laughed. "I hope so, too. He looked kinda cute, though. I don't really want him to get into trouble. Still, it isn't like we avoided him on purpose—or needed him in the first place. I mean, we're sixteen now. And who do our parents think will be on this train anyway?"

"Count Dracula?" I suggested. "We *do* go through Transylvania tonight."

"Yeah, right. I'm *so* afraid."

We contemplated our pleasant predicament and decided to play chess all night, beginning at once. Hannah rummaged around in her backpack and pulled out her well-used travel set.

"I have been beating my dad recently," she said, setting up. "And I am *so* ready to beat you."

"In your dreams, Hannah. Succeeding at chess requires a male mind. Winning takes strategy, not sappy emotion. I *have* let you win some in the past, but—"

At that she tossed an empty Coke can in the direction of my head. I deftly caught it and returned it in the same fashion.

"Good catch, Con. You should stick to activities where you use your arm, not your head."

Actually, beating her at chess was like beating her at anything—very hard and very rare.

We played a leisurely game, more focused on our vacation than on our chess. There would be endless hours of skiing, no parents to answer to, and best of all, we would be away from our least favorite teacher, who had just been elevated to principal. Ms. Gaul had always suspected us of every prank played at the American International School, and now she could haul us into the principal's office to discuss each one.

Hannah was looking happier than she had since the start of school. We had both come back from exciting summer vacations in America and were neither one too happy to be back in Europe attending school again. But things had started looking up a month ago after she got an invitation to visit her aunt and uncle at their new diplomatic post in Romania. And the Goldbergs had agreed she could bring a friend. I smiled.

We were on our way to a city so remote I had never heard of it—couldn't even pronounce it. And thanks to Andrew Hart, we were on our own!

"Do you think the poor guy will call or email Uncle Aaron and tell him what happened, or try for one good night of sleep before he admits to missing the train?" Hannah was beginning to sound concerned for him. "Uncle Aaron and Aunt Ruth are going to feel responsible and worry big-time. And Aunt Ruth . . . well, she does tend to hover."

"Oh no, not a hoverer! I hate hoverers. And in that case I think the 'poor guy,' as you call him, should probably write his resignation, fax it to Uncle Aaron, then jump off one of those cool stone bridges in Budapest and get it over with."

Hannah didn't seem to appreciate my humor.

"Oh please, Hannah, stop looking so pathetic," I went on. "Andrew Hart will be fine. Our parents, however, would not be fine if they knew we were on this train alone." I shifted into my mom's voice: " 'Con, you and Hannah cannot set off alone into the dead of a winter night to a remote region of a desolate country, traveling over the snowy Carpathian Mountains into some horrible winter storm in which you could get stranded for hours or days by yourselves and all alone and, Nigel, do you really think this is a good idea?' " I stopped, gasping for breath.

Hannah was cracking up at my impersonation. "You sound just like her. You haven't lost your touch, Con, and your mother has become a bit of a hoverer, too, since our Zürich experience and your brush with the black widow spider last summer. Maybe she's decided you are a menace to yourself and others. . . ." Hannah paused. "Maybe your mom has a point."

I ignored Hannah's barb. But as if to prove Mom's point, the train jerked forward then, throwing me back against the hard seat, grinding to a halt with the squeal of metal on metal before the engine managed to recover and began inching forward again—like it couldn't make up its mind.

"If only my mom could see us now," I said as snow swirled around the grimy window in the darkness. "Alone in this desolate wasteland—the whole dark-and-stormy-night thing, with the snowy Carpathian Mountains dead ahead."

"Okay, okay, Con, enough already. You *are* starting to scare me." Hannah brushed aside the flimsy orange curtain that didn't quite cover the glass door separating us from the corridor. "And if this is first class, I would hate to see coach on the Bucharest Express," she added, wiping a thick layer of dirt off the glass.

"Oh no!" Hannah jumped back from the glass, gasping at the sight of black eyes, set above a scruffy beard and long, bulbous nose, staring back at her. Behind the burly, not-so-friendly face were three other men huddled around our door looking in. Each was loaded down with bulging plastic bags and hand-wrapped parcels. "Con, can't you lock the door or something?" Hannah hissed under her breath.

I rolled my eyes at my naïve friend. "It doesn't lock, Hannah. It's a train compartment, not your house. These guys may have tickets, too."

There was room for six in each first-class carriage—no reason we wouldn't have company.

The pink in Hannah's cheeks turned to white at the thought of sharing the next twelve hours with the rough-looking men still standing outside our door. Maybe it wasn't so cool that Andrew Hart missed the train, after all, I thought fleetingly. We could use him about now.

"Do something, Con," Hannah whispered as the man in front slid the door open and stepped inside, his friends close behind. The smell of garlic, cigarette smoke, and alcohol flooded into the room with them.

I jumped to my feet and found my six-foot frame more than matched his height. Muscle was another matter. He had bulk to back his icy gaze. Hoping all my warm winter clothing would hide the fact that working on my grandfather's ranch last summer had not produced much mass, I bluffed. Hey, when you don't have it, don't admit it!

It had worked before. I moved in front of the men, blocking their way before they could drop their bags or sit down.

Shoulders squared, I demanded to know, in German, if they had tickets for this compartment. Waving my ticket in case he couldn't understand German—which seemed fairly likely since we were in Hungary on a train bound for Romania—I kept up the pressure, hoping the men would leave. My guess was they didn't have a first-class ticket and were playing their own game of bluff.

The man's bleary eyes looked confused, and the others started jabbering in something other than English or German, my only two languages. They didn't seem to be able to produce a ticket—which I kept demanding—and finally but not happily they backed away.

Hannah tugged the curtain back over most of the window, I propped my boot against the door handle and any more surprise visitors, and we hoped for the best.

"Ugh! The thought of spending the rest of the night with them . . ." Hannah shuddered, nervously fingering her necklace. A Bas Mitzva gift from her grandmother, the delicate mezuzah always hung around Hannah's neck. She tended to finger it when nervous. "Maybe some nice little Hungarian ladies will join us," she said, rubbing the raised Hebrew letters on the mezuzah's little gold door.

Trying not to think about who might be on the train, we kicked back and began to focus on our second game of chess. Hannah opened with one of her usual bold moves, and I concentrated hard, determined not to start this trip by losing to her twice.

Absorbed in the game, we didn't notice the tap at first. Then it came again.

"Don't look now, Hannah, but we have company."

A Gypsy family was gathered around the door. There were two women, faces framed with bright red scarves, surveying us. A scrawny little boy held up a dirty hand, cupped and pleading. Behind them a big man wearing a broad-brimmed black felt hat continued tapping on the glass, demanding we give to the boy.

"I told you not to look," I said to Hannah, who stared at the little boy.

"Maybe we should help them," she ventured.

I shook my head—at her and at them—with my foot still firmly planted against the door. Finally the man, shaking his fist and shouting, took his family and moved on down the swaying corridor.

"Whew, that was close."

"But maybe we *should* have given the little boy something," Hannah protested. "It was an opportunity for a real mitzvah, and I missed it."

"Mitzvah, schmitzva. Your soft heart will get you into trouble, Hannah. Remember, our parents warned us about beggars who might be con artists. Save your good deeds for me. Now, *that* would be a real mitzvah."

Hannah went on worrying, and I went on trying to beat her at chess. I tossed my backpack on top of my skis on the metal luggage rack overhead and stretched out.

Between moves, Hannah set about cleaning up. She brushed all the cigarette ash from the previous occupants off the seat and straightened the red seat covers, generally messing with my concentration.

"You don't have to clean, Hannah. We're not going to live here." I was amazed at her female ability to focus on the totally unimportant.

It was still cold, and the dim light bulb tended to flicker when we went around corners, but we didn't much care. We were out of school and headed for great skiing.

"Tell me again why your aunt and uncle are in Ice and not Bucharest?"

"Con, you moron, it's pronounced *Yahsh*, not *ice*. And I explained all this before. Weren't you listening?"

We both knew the answer to that one, so I didn't bother to reply.

I took out the remainder of my bag of roasted chestnuts and polished off the few remaining morsels. Bits of sausage were mixed with the nuts. I offered the bag to Hannah.

She wrinkled her nose in disgust at the congealed greasy mess and explained once again why her aunt and uncle were going to be in Iasi instead of at the embassy in Bucharest.

"Listen up this time, Con. On Friday the Romanian government is unveiling a statue in Iasi of some old fascist leader—Marshal Ion Antonescu. He was prime minister during World War II. And they invited the ambassador to the ceremony—"

"I hope *we* don't have to go," I interrupted. "I hate to mix politics and fun."

"You hate to mix anything with your fun, Con. No, of course they aren't going. Pay attention. Romania was an ally with Germany in World War II. Antonescu liked Hitler so much that he tried to be like him. He came to power with the help of his own version of Hitler's SS—a brutal fascist organization called the Iron Guard. And they set about—quite successfully, I might add—to rid Romania of its Jews. It was awful, and no American ambassador would turn up to honor him, especially not Uncle Aaron."

Hannah paused, struggling with the painful history of her Jewish heritage in Europe. I knew there was nothing I could say and waited for her to go on.

"Well, anyway, Uncle Aaron thinks the current government built this statue just to please some radical fascist elements in the country. So of course he turned down the invitation."

"Isn't that a little like the German government building a statute of Hitler and inviting the Americans to rally around and cheer?"

"Ten points, Con! But Uncle Aaron still wants to be close enough to check it out. He thinks outside neo-Nazi groups plan to use this event to stir up trouble in Romania, which has enough problems already. And Aunt Ruth wanted to visit Iasi anyway. It's the old capital of Moldova and famous for its beautiful monasteries and stuff like that. And we can all go skiing there, so, voilà! A holiday in Iasi."

Hannah pulled a map out of her backpack. Uncle Aaron had marked our route and circled Iasi.

"Look, dummy, learn something," she said. "We are here crossing Hungary now." She ran her finger across the Great Hungarian Plain. "And this is where we will cross into Romania—sometime in the wee hours of the morning, I think." She pointed to the tiny black letters of the border town of Oradea.

"Okay," I said, getting into this at last. "We cross into Romania at Oradea, which is located in . . . isn't this fascinating . . . Tran-syl-van-ia." I rolled the *r* and drew out the name. "Now, that is just the kind of place you want to go in the dead of night on a broken-down old train." I smiled a Dracula kind of smile, revealing my teeth.

"Save it, Con. I don't think the train goes anywhere near the castle of Prince Vlad "the Impaler" Dracul. He was much scarier than the Dracula myth about him, by the way."

I hated it when she did that—knew more than I did and didn't scare easily.

"Through Transylvania," she continued, tracing our route. "Then we go over the Carpathian Mountains your mom's so worried about and should arrive on the other side, in Iasi, by noon tomorrow, barring any snowstorms. It takes twelve hours."

Iasi, I noticed, was only a few miles from Moldova, once

part of the Ukraine, once part of Russia. These people couldn't seem to make up their minds.

"It *better* have good skiing," I declared. "I'm not going to any old monasteries. And I've seen enough castles in Austria to last a lifetime. And I *was* looking forward to staying at the embassy in Bucharest . . . with banquets each night, servants to wait on us, that kind of thing. It'd be awesome to be treated as a VIP for two weeks."

"You *always* want to be treated like a VIP."

"True. Do you think they'll have all the perks in Iasi?" I ignored her sarcasm. "And more important, are they bringing an American cook?"

"Do you ever stop thinking about your stomach?" Hannah made a face at me. "The sight of you eating that cold grease is making me sick." She pulled out another can of Coke and tossed it to me—more gently this time. "At least wash the stuff down."

I drank the Coke, wishing afterward for a nice cup of hot chocolate, but otherwise utterly content.

Hannah had a distant, worried look and admitted when pressed that a bunch of neo-Nazis coming together to celebrate wasn't her idea of holiday resort atmosphere.

"I've seen enough of *them* to last a lifetime," she said. "And with Dirty Harry and the others on the loose . . . it gives me the creeps."

Dirty Harry. I wished she hadn't mentioned his name.

It gave me the creeps, too, but I didn't admit it. One month ago Hans Grunwald, still Dirty Harry to me, had escaped from prison—with a little help from his skinhead friends. The police in Vienna had assured the Goldbergs and my parents that they were watching every possible entry point into Austria and that there was no way he could even get close to us. Everyone worried anyway. I figured that was why my folks had agreed to this trip to Romania: It was sufficiently far away from Vienna and Dirty Harry, should he choose to come looking for us. I did find it comforting to know that *only* our parents, Uncle Aaron, Aunt Ruth, and Andrew Hart knew our location at the moment.

Still, being certain that there was no way Dirty Harry could know that Hannah and I were alone in the middle of the night on a train bound for nowhere didn't keep the shivers from running down my spine when I thought about him on the loose. I had not forgotten his promise to me that night on the boat in Zürich—his promise to find me and kill me for making a fool out of him in front of his friends. He had repeated it again with his eyes when Hannah and I testified against him at the trial in Zürich. Our testimony sealed his fate. And now I knew he would like to seal mine. For good.

"Maybe it wouldn't have been so bad to have Andrew Hart along with us after all," Hannah said, her laughter long gone, replaced by a deep frown.

"Who needs him? Hans Grunwald can't find us here. And besides, you have me to protect you. I kept those men out of here, didn't I?"

"Whatever, Con. I think I'll just stay awake all night. Want another game?"

With one bold stroke I took her rook early on and nearly won, only to be whacked decisively in the next game. She was ruthless.

"You must learn to bring out your queen earlier and sacrifice a few pawns to get what you want," Hannah said, looking very sleepy and only slightly smug. Her ski jacket still on and her long legs bent to fit on the seat, Hannah tucked a couple of sweaters over her jeans as a blanket. Her eyes began to close.

I was beginning to feel a little sleepy myself.

"I'm just resting my eyes for a few minutes, but I won't go to sleep. I promise. We'll play another game in a minute. . . ." She drifted off.

So much for staying awake all night, I thought. Digging

through my backpack for a *Road and Track* magazine, I found instead an unopened letter from Frau Rozstoski, which had arrived today. I had tossed it in my bag and forgotten it till now.

The envelope was bulging. *What on earth?* I wondered. I was accustomed to getting brief notes from my very old friend, but never long letters. The flowery script, written in coal black ink on tissue-thin light blue pages, was just like Mia Rozstoski: old-fashioned and classy.

A thousand-schilling note was folded in the pages, and it dropped onto my lap.

"Yahoo!" I half shouted, always happy to have a little extra cash. Glad my outburst hadn't awakened Hannah, I tucked the Austrian money, worth about seventy U.S. dollars, into my pocket and proceeded to read the first of many pages.

> *My dearest Con,*
> *I can no longer call you my "littlest angel" since you are no longer little, and probably not as angelic as you once were! If I know you, and I think I do, you will not read this letter until you are on the train.*

"You do know me, Mia," I whispered to myself, smiling.

> *I hope you are enjoying the ride! How I wish I could be there with you. I have not been back to my home since that day in 1942 when I was taken away by the Iron Guard soldiers. I long to see my home once more. Even though I know I will never be well enough to go back, I dream of it still and wonder about so many things.*
> *You may not be my littlest angel anymore, yet you do remain the light of my life, and it has given me great pleasure to watch you grow tall and handsome, clever and witty. You have always brought me joy, Constantine—ever since you and your mother moved into the apartment next to mine in Grossgmain all those years ago.*
> *You have done a lot of growing up lately, and I know*

last year it was hard for you to learn about Herr Donner and his war crimes. But in the end you accepted the truth, and I am proud of you for that. I am also proud of how you helped your grandparents in Wyoming last summer— and learned to appreciate the spiritual inheritance passed down to you by godly grandparents. So you are truly grow- ing up, and because you are not a little boy anymore, I have a favor to ask of you. I do not want to burden you with anything that will take time away from your ski holiday with Hannah, yet I must ask.

I have told you many stories about my life in Barsa on our beautiful estate called Livada de Meri, which means a place of apples. *It was named for the vast orchards that surround the house. But I have never told you about what happened on that last and fateful day in my beloved Li- vada de Meri. I have never told anyone* all *of it before.*

"Oh no," I groaned, dropping the letter onto the seat and looking at Hannah, who was still sleeping peacefully. "I don't want to know," I whispered to myself.

A heavy feeling came over me, reaching down to the pit of my stomach. Hannah, had she been awake, would have told me it was from all the grease I had just consumed. But she would be wrong. Something about Frau R.'s letter made me nervous. I didn't want to learn what happened on that "fateful day" or what favor it would lead her to ask of me. I stared into the darkness slipping by outside the train, and somehow it got inside my head, overwhelming me. I was lulled into last year by the *clickety, clickety, clack* of the train and the swaying along the tracks. The memories of last year and all it had exposed came rushing back to me. Grossgmain. Frau Rozstoski. Herr Donner and Dirty Harry. All of it, and the faces of men who hated Hannah for her race, were intrud- ing unwanted on my holiday.

I tried to think instead about our Romanian holiday. But in the blackness of my mood, Mom's words came back to me as I looked around the shabby train.

She had explained to me how Communism and Nicolae Ceausescu, the dictator who ruled Romania with a corrupt iron fist up until 1989, had left the Romanian people in poverty, the country in ruins, way behind western Europe. When the people finally rose up against Ceausescu and his wife, Elena, there was a brief but bloody revolution. Then the dictator and his wife were executed on live television, Christmas Day 1989. Mom had also warned me that, thanks to Ceausescu, I should expect poverty and primitive conditions in the country he had ruled. I, however, expected to ski all day, be treated like a VIP, and not go chasing old memories for Frau R.

The dim light bulb kept flickering, adding to the uneasy feeling in my stomach. I closed my eyes, trying to imagine a ski slope. But all I could see was the image of a sunny apartment in Grossgmain belonging to an elegant old lady, and her sweet face watching me devour her special homemade chocolate ice cream. The same elegant old lady who, years ago in a Romanian prison, had been beaten so severely that to this day she could barely walk.

A favor, her letter said, a favor that might intrude. I loved Frau Rozstoski like a grandma, almost as much as I loved Grandpa and Gran Walker, but I felt tired of old people and their problems right now. I was tired of the past. Tired of other people's history getting in my present. I picked up the delicate pages of her letter, holding them loosely, wishing they would float out the window unread. I considered opening the window but knew that I wouldn't.

"Okay, okay," I whispered begrudgingly. "As long as whatever it is doesn't interfere with my fun. . . ." I raised the letter to my now tired eyes.

It was a time to die, not *a time to be born. . . .*

29

A TIME TO DIE

*"There is a time for everything, a season for every activity under heaven. A time to be born and a time to die...."
So says the book of Ecclesiastes, and that winter in Europe was a time to die. Yet in the midst of such danger had been born a beautiful baby.*

I read on despite myself, transported to that long-ago time at Frau Rozstoski's beloved Livada de Meri on the banks of the Prut River.

I was standing in the drawing room when Gabriel Levi, my friend and the manager of the estate, told me of the birth of his first child, a boy, eight days earlier. But there was pain as well as pride in his face, for he, too, knew this was not the time for a Jewish child to be born. In that winter of 1942, the prime minister of Romania, Ion Antonescu, had his Iron Guard out rounding up Jewish people for "transport" to camps.

Forgive me, Con, but I must back up and explain. I know I have told you many stories of my life in Moldova, which is the territory where Livada de Meri was situated. But I am not sure how much you remember; you were never much for sitting still.

Livada de Meri was given to my father, Count Laszlo Rozstoski, for service rendered the Austrian crown. My mother was half Italian royalty and half Austrian aristoc-

racy. She belonged to the Hapsburg family and grew up in Vienna. She loved "society," and so for her, the estate in Moldova was more of a curse than a blessing since it required living on the outer rim of the Austro-Hungarian Empire, nearly in the Ukraine. But for me it was the most beautiful spot in the world. When I was a little girl, I loved traveling with my father over the rolling hills and through the dense woods, watching him as he managed our vast lands and businesses. We owned the mill and the timber, apple and cherry orchards, herds of sheep and cattle. Most of the people who lived in the nearby town of Barsa worked for my father in one of our industries.

What I did not like so much was moving to our city house in Vienna for the "social season," which lasted three long months. I hated the stuffy parlor parties and dressing up every day. The noisy bells of Saint Stephen's Cathedral pealed day and night and made me miss the quiet of the woods.

My mother was horrified that I didn't love her world of parties, and she blamed my father for introducing me to business and the land, the world of men, which she considered below my station and class. I did enjoy the music, art, and architecture of Vienna, but no matter how hard she tried, I couldn't become the socialite my mother had hoped for. I loved the energy and excitement of Livada de Meri. I was fourteen when my baby brother, Michael, the son and heir, was born. But by then my father so enjoyed taking me with him as he managed the estate that I continued to spend every possible minute on the land—even though I couldn't legally inherit it. My mother insisted on bringing me the best tutors from all over Europe. From them I learned my lessons in English, German, French, and Russian.

Like the rest of Europe's nobility, we lived our privileged lives, largely unaware of the coming storm. Oh, we knew there was some political unrest—even as a girl I could tell from my father's conversations. But we really had no idea that the life we knew was soon to be no more.

I could see the river from my second-story bedroom window, as our stone mansion sat on a slight rise overlooking the wide water of the Prut River, which ran along the northern boundary of Livada de Meri. It was also the border separating the Austro-Hungarian Empire from the Russian Ukraine. (Today it separates Romania and Moldova.) The river had fascinated and terrified me for as long as I could remember. I could see the Ukrainian soldiers manning a small border post on the bridge between the countries.

Sometimes I had nightmares about soldiers crossing the river to kill me. My father would assure me that no soldiers would stand a chance against the mighty Austro-Hungarian Empire. "Like a mosquito on an elephant," he would say to me, "a mere annoyance."

But late in the summer of 1914, the "mosquito" roared, and before that dreadful day was over, my father was dead, our beautiful possessions were destroyed, and the apple orchards by the house were stripped of all their bright red fruit. My mother managed to escape with me and Michael to our house in Vienna, where we lived for the duration of World War I. And four years later when that terrible war was over, the "elephant" was dead, carved up into little countries. The mighty Austro-Hungarian Empire was no more, and Livada de Meri had become part of Romania.

After the war I was determined to return home, despite my mother's protests. Michael was still young and stayed with our mother in Vienna. Even years later he had no desire to live on or manage the estate and was happy to let me attempt to rebuild our fortune before he claimed it. When I arrived I was shocked by the condition of the house and lands: fields overgrown, the mill in ruins, our herds of sheep and cattle eaten by hungry armies. The iron gates still stood guard at the end of the lane, but our home's splendor was only a memory. The woods were wild and lawless, inhabited by bandits.

But I had learned much at my father's side and slowly began to rebuild. Twenty years later the estate was beginning to prosper—not back to its former glory, but on the way. My hope was that Europe had learned the lessons of war and would let people live in peace.

My hope was in vain. In 1941, when Romania joined forces with Hitler against Russia, it was only a matter of time before the Rozstoski estate would once again be in the path of war. I had not forgotten what had happened to my father, and I kept promising my mother and Michael that I would join them in the safety of Vienna long before the enemy once again crossed the Prut River.

What I didn't tell my mother, Con, and what I have never told another soul, was that I had much more to worry about from the Romanian Iron Guard than from any foreign soldiers. The prime minister of Romania, Marshal Ion Antonescu, in making a military alliance with Germany, had agreed to follow Nazi policy by destroying the Romanian Jewish population, citizens who had lived in Romania for centuries. On June 29, 1941, Antonescu ordered a massacre in Iasi, leaving thousands of Jewish men, women, and children dead by the hand of the Iron Guard soldiers. The rest of the Jewish community went into hiding, some at Livada de Meri.

Among these fugitives was Gabriel Levi. When Gabriel brought me news of his newborn son, he was dressed, as always, in his drab, woolen clothes. But underneath the peasant disguise beat the heart of a master musician. Before the war I had heard him play piano in the most prestigious music salons in Iasi. He had also been a respected professor of music, and I had listened to many of his lectures at the university, speaking with him personally on several occasions.

After the 1941 massacre, Gabriel and his wife, Rachel, came to me for a place to hide. It was the least I could do. Gabriel helped me run the estate, and we somehow managed to increase production in that troubled half year. Gabriel took in every wandering Jew looking for a place to hide and turned them into productive workers at Livada de Meri. I had yeshiva teachers working in the mill, Jewish *schoolgirls picking apples, musicians herding sheep.*

    *Gabriel proved to be more than a capable manager—
he became my friend. He came to the house every day to
complete estate business, and afterward we talked of things
that had been part of our lives during better times: art,
literature, music. Soon I couldn't bear the thought of returning to Vienna and leaving Gabriel and the others to
the mercy of the Iron Guard. I miss him to this day and
wonder what became of his newborn son. That is the reason
for this long letter. But I get ahead of myself. You must be
patient with an old lady telling her story, Con.*

I wasn't as patient as Frau R. might have hoped, but my
foot was falling asleep and I stopped reading to shift positions.
Somewhat comfortable once again, I returned to the letter.

    *"What will you do, Gabriel?" I asked him that morn-
ing, shocked at his news. "This is no time for a baby to be
born." The local Iron Guard leader, a most disagreeable
man by the name of Andrei Popa, was sending his men to
search the estate more and more frequently. I knew they suspected that not all of my peasants were really farm laborers.
Still, they had no proof. But as a single woman, I couldn't
hide a baby. I didn't even know how much longer I could
hide any of the adults.*

    "How will you protect your son?" I demanded of him.

    *For an answer he took off his wide-brimmed black hat
and tipped his head to reveal a yarmulke underneath.
"What I am going to do," he said, "is take my son, now
eight days old, to his bris. Circumcision is the sign and seal
of his place in Judaism. He is a son of the covenant, and I
will not deny him his spiritual heritage, no matter the danger."*

    I recall Gabriel's handsome face beaming with pride.

    *Instead of congratulating him, though, I shouted at
him for endangering us all by wearing a yarmulke. There
was, I think, a pleading in his eyes as he replied that he
could not possibly go to the mohel, who would circumcise his*

son, with his head uncovered. For this particular mohel was also a rabbi. Then he explained that the rabbi was nearby—in fact, was at that moment guarding my front gate.

We seldom discussed Gabriel's hiring practices, as it was safer for me not to know. But I was a little surprised by the news that I was employing a respected rabbi from Iasi as the keeper of my gate.

Gabriel laughed when he told me about the rabbi. Taking my hand in his, he said, "I didn't tell you about my new son in order to ask for help; I came to tell you my good news. I want you to be glad for me . . . and Rachel. Someday when all this is over, we will bring our son here to meet you so he can thank you for what you have done for all of us. Jews have known tyrants before; Hitler and Antonescu are simply the latest in a long line. And you are wrong. It is a time to be born. Today my son will officially be given his name. While it is not customary to name a child after a living relative—lest the angel of death become confused—given the circumstances, we have chosen to call our son Gabriel. I pray that one of us will survive to carry on the name."

Con, I can remember as if it were yesterday, looking out the diamond-shaped panes of glass at the birch trees alongside the lane. I was afraid for him, his wife, and his newborn son.

He tried to comfort me. "A wise rabbi once taught me a lesson from the book of Job," he told me. "It is not in our power to explain either the tranquility of the wicked or the sufferings of the upright. I see in the very birth of my son a defeat for the wicked who would destroy us. The Scriptures tell us that what the locusts have eaten God will restore."

His words did not comfort me. I was very angry that he could stand there calmly discussing moral enigmas when his son's life was at stake. When all of our lives were at stake.

I reminded Gabriel what we both knew about the train transports that had carried almost every Jew in Iasi away to the "camps" from which no one ever returned. "So how," I asked him, "do you propose to save your son?"

I have never forgotten his answer.

"God will provide a way," he said to me. "After all, God has provided you."

I wanted to tell him his trust was misplaced, that I could not protect him much longer. I wanted to pound on the window and cry at the unfairness of it all. Then I remembered one last treasure that I could give his son on this important day. A gift that might save his life.

I ran up the center hall staircase to the second-floor west wing, into my bedroom. I heard gunfire in the distance, which made me rush to the bedside stand where I kept my books and few remaining treasures.

From the back of the top drawer, I pulled out the last really valuable item at Livada de Meri. It was a rare book, a copy of the Psalms given to me by my father. I sat down on my bed to hold the precious book one last time. The leather binding was still soft, the gold leaf that covered the edges still shiny.

I held it in my hands, between my thumb and index finger. As my father had shown me when he gave it to me, I fanned the fore edge of the book. As I did so, a delicate painting hidden underneath the gold appeared. It was an original watercolor of Livada de Meri in the spring, with white blossoms hanging on the apple trees, sunlight sparkling on the hundreds of diamond-shaped windows set in the stone facade of our house, and the Carpathian Mountains looming in the background. A little girl sat reading a book under the shade of a tall birch tree. That little girl was me.

Tears ran down my cheeks as I held the book, wondering how it was possible I could still miss my father so much.

My father and Gabriel were the only two men in my life who had treated me as an intellectual equal, who had shared my love for the land and the wonders of art and music and books. I had lost the one and was about to lose the other.

I hesitated only long enough to remember my father's words when he gave this gift to me.

"I cannot give you my estate, Mia. That will go some-day to your brother, Michael. But as long as you have this book, you will have a little of Livada de Meri, too."

The picture under the gold leaf was signed by the master French painter Didot Freres, who had come all the way to the edge of the empire to put one of his masterpieces on the fore edge of my book.

"Keep it always," my father had said. "And remember."

I turned to the final page and read the last line of Psalm 150:

"Let every thing that hath breath praise the Lord. Praise ye the Lord."

Quickly now, as I was sure there was more gunfire in the distance, I dipped my quill pen in a bottle of black ink and wrote on that last page underneath those inspired words a few of my own:

"For Gabriel Levi, son of my friend, born January 17 in the year of our Lord 1942. Maria Rozstoski."

I blew the ink dry, closed the covers of the book, and ran back to Gabriel, afraid the gunfire might mean Iron Guard soldiers had come again to search. If so, they would find the "peasant" in my drawing room wearing a yarmulke, and Gabriel would miss his son's bris and probably the rest of his life.

Gabriel had heard the gunshots, too, and was heading for the back door, which led under the stairs out into the orchard behind the house. From there he could hide in the woods that stretched down to the river or in one of the sheds by the dock.

"Wait," I called to him. "I have something for your son."

We heard the sound of voices, and if I had known they were so near I would not have detained him. Oh, Con, I have longed my whole life to go back and change that morning. But I kept him there and showed him the book, spreading the pages to reveal the painting. He protested taking such a precious gift from me. I reminded him there were *people who could be bribed to take and hide a child as their own. The book might give his son such a chance. It was an offer he couldn't refuse.*

"Thank you, Mia," he said, using my familiar name for the first time and kissing me on both cheeks. Clasping the book to his chest, he headed for the little door under the stairs as Andrei Popa's iron-toed boots kicked open the front door. A half dozen soldiers under his command followed him into my hall. As they approached, Gabriel moved protectively in front of me.

"Get out of my way, peasant. My business is with the lady of the manor."

The drunken commander shoved Gabriel out of the way. As he did so, I whispered to Gabriel to go.

Every detail of the next few moments is etched upon my mind. There was a smell of stale smoke and strong drink on the men, and I recognized the smell of gunpowder and hot metal from recently fired weapons.

"Take what you came for and get out," I told the men, gesturing to the few things still left in the nearly empty house. They had come before, questioning me and stealing whatever caught their fancy, knowing I could not protest. Little was left to take.

Andrei Popa grinned at me, his yellow teeth showing years of neglect.

"This time I came for you," he said, his boots clicking on the broad black-and-white tiles that had covered the floor since I was a child.

"Did you think the pathetic old man by your gate could protect you?" He waved his pistol around, blowing on the end of it like it was a game.

"No . . ." Gabriel groaned, realizing what the soldier meant.

There was a moment of confusion as the soldiers joined their leader in laughter at the stunned faces before them.

I pleaded again for Gabriel to go before it was too late.

But it was already too late. Popa lurched toward me, his pistol still drawn, and Gabriel moved between us once again. It triggered some madness in the commander, and he fired for no other reason than for the annoyance of someone standing in his way.

As Gabriel's big body gave way, his hat tumbled off, rolling across the floor, revealing what Andrei Popa had been trying for months to prove: Maria Rozstoski was hiding Jews.

Triumphant now, the man reached down to pull me off the body of my dying friend. As he did so, a glint of gold caught his eye. He pried my book out of Gabriel's fingers and shoved it inside his stinking jacket before dragging me away.

I have never been back to Livada de Meri. First prison, then years of Communist control prevented me from travel. Now my feeble body has kept me from returning.

Con, will you go back and see my home for me? I am very old, almost as old as the century that has passed, a century stained with blood. And there is one more favor I would ask. Before I die, I would like to know the fate of Gabriel's son. Did he live to carry on the Levi name? Inquire, my clever young friend, of people you meet who might recall what transpired with these people when the war was over. My heart is riding with you on that train as it carries you to the place where I was young.

With love, Frau R.

TOP SECRET

3

THE BORDER

"Con, wake up! You're screaming."

I opened my eyes and to my great relief found Hannah, not the Iron Guard, shaking me. I was in a train compartment, not Frau Rozstoski's drawing room, and no body of Gabriel Levi lay bleeding on the floor.

"Boy, am I glad to see you," I mumbled rather foolishly, trying to shake the feeling of terror. The pale blue pages of Frau R.'s letter had scattered onto the floor. I had fallen asleep, and the terror of Livada de Meri had turned into a nightmare of my own. My mouth was dry, my legs cramped, and train travel was already feeling not so good.

"Really glad to see it's only you," I said again through the fog in my brain.

Hannah gave me that raised-eyebrow-head-tilted-down look that I knew so well. And she didn't even bother to say, "Who'd ya expect, dummy?"

I stretched my stiff muscles and looked around at the dingy surroundings, trying to shake off the feeling that fascist thugs were about to turn up looking for Frau R. and her friend Gabriel. As the train began to slow down, I scratched frost off the window with my arm to see if we were at the border. I got only a dirty sleeve for my trouble—that and a glimpse of darkness still rushing by in a sea of swirling snow.

"So much for the view," I complained to Hannah. "What time is it, anyway? And don't they heat these things?"

"It's nearly two-thirty, and no, I don't think so. I'm still freezing. Who were you fighting in your dream? It looked like you were losing. Worse than you lose at chess. But don't worry," she added, "you didn't drool or anything."

"Thanks, Hannah, so kind of you to tell me."

"Well, your dream was really something," she went on. "You were thrashing around and shouting, 'No . . . no!' Of course, it could have been the sausage and roasted chestnuts."

The train interrupted Hannah at that moment with a sudden and not very smooth stop, throwing me back and Hannah forward. Glad for a chance to end the conversation, I got up and dropped the window, leaning out to look up and down the track at passengers boarding at the Romanian border town.

A street lamp dimly lit the platform in front of the little station building with *Oradea* written in bold letters over the door. Border guards with German shepherd dogs patrolled the area, checking the papers of people getting on and off.

A group of men huddled against the building out of the wind and snow, waiting to get on, their faces hid by shadows. I lost interest and with one mighty heave sent the rusty window back up into place.

"Anyone interesting getting on?" Hannah asked, not sounding terribly interested.

"Nope, doesn't look like it," I replied.

A mouse scampered across the floor, from underneath my seat through a hole under Hannah's.

"Con, was that what I think it was?" She pulled her feet up onto the seat.

"Yup. Probably lives on crumbs dropped from passengers."

"Well, he wisely chose your side of the car," Hannah said

calmly. "I don't hate mice, but I don't intend to sleep with one under my seat, either."

"No problem."

I pulled a ski pole down and started poking it through the hole.

"Careful," she complained. "I don't want a mouse-kabob—"

Before she could finish her sentence, the door opened and a heavyset man in a blue uniform motioned me to get up off the floor and produce our papers. His muzzled German shepherd pulled against the leash, drooling through the mesh. The dog probably smelled the mouse but, trained to look for drugs not rodents, quickly lost interest in exploring under the seat.

I'm sure the border guard wondered what I had been doing on the floor, but he didn't stay to inquire and moved on after a quick look at our passports.

"Here," I said to Hannah, handing her the letter. "It wasn't the food that gave me nightmares. It was this, and I think you should read it while we wait."

Always curious, she took the folded sheets of Frau R.'s letter that I had picked up off the floor. The thousand-schilling note was in my jacket pocket.

I listened to the sounds of the guard and his dog moving down the row of compartments in our train car. Wishing they would hurry so we could get going again, I watched Hannah read.

She was so engrossed in the letter, she wouldn't have noticed if the mouse climbed into her lap. I watched her face grow still and her eyes mist over. Finally, when she came to the last of the thin blue sheets of paper, she laid them in her lap and looked at me, a sadness in her eyes.

"It's the same all over again," she said, shaking her head. "Over and over again, all over Europe. The same hatred of us, the same cowards murdering men, women, and . . . and probably that little baby."

"I know. I'm sorry, Hannah."

"I wonder what happened to him, Con."

"Don't even think about it, Hannah. Frau R.'s request is crazy! How could we find Livada de Meri, let alone people who might remember what is now ancient history? She's old, doesn't have a clue what she's asking."

"She is old, Con. But she is far from not knowing what she's asking. All she wants us to do is ask a few questions—see if anyone remembers what happened to the Levi family and to Gabriel's son. How hard can that be?"

I was afraid she was going to say that.

"How hard, Hannah? Get real. If the baby lived—which he probably did not—he would be . . ." I paused, trying to do the math.

"Close to sixty now, Einstein. So what? There must be someone left in Barsa or Iasi who remembers the Levi family. Maybe the baby grew up to be a musician like his father. Maybe we can find the university where Gabriel Levi taught. At the very least we can go to Livada de Meri and take pictures for her. It sounds so beautiful, so romantic!"

Hannah was really getting into this. I saw our days on the slope dwindling as we ran around trying to solve a very old—and very impossible—mystery.

I tried reason.

"Yeah, sure, we can go take a picture of her estate, which is probably rubble now. But, Hannah, we can't find Gabriel's family. They *didn't* survive. That's the point. I'm sorry, but it's been more than half a century since the murder, and his son and his wife probably died in the Holocaust like most of the other Jews. . . ." I stopped as her face clouded over again. "I'm sorry, Hannah, but you know it's true. What's the chance they survived?"

Silently Hannah glared at me.

"Okay, we don't know for sure they didn't survive." I crumbled under the weight of her penetrating stare. "But we don't have a car, we don't speak Romanian. . . . What does Frau R. expect us to do, find the book?"

"It would be nice."

"Hannah! Get serious! And besides, we have something more important to do than run around looking for some old Romanian man. Like ski and have fun."

Hannah got quiet again.

I stared out the glass partition into the corridor, thinking about the lovely time we would have had if Frau R. hadn't written that letter.

That's when I saw him.

"Duck, Hannah," I hissed, grabbing her arm and pulling her off the seat. She tumbled on top of me as I hit the cold metal floor.

"Have you gone crazy . . . again?" she asked, struggling to get up.

"Keep your head down! I mean it. Dirty Harry just walked past."

"That's not funny, Con, not funny at all." She pounded me on the arm with her fist, really angry. "Let me up."

But for once in my life, I wasn't trying to be funny.

"Please, please keep your head down," I said, holding on. "It . . . it was him. Dirty Harry. Hans Grunwald. He was with another man I didn't recognize, but . . ." I was having trouble breathing. Desperate to make her believe me, I described his dark coat and hat pulled down over his eyes. The same swaggering walk.

"It was him, Hannah, the same walk, stalking like . . . like a hunter. And I saw his face, at least partially. You've got to believe me. And you've got to keep your head down. Please."

My heart was pumping too much blood. I could feel it racing in my chest, pounding in my head. Hannah, who knows me well, could see now I wasn't kidding.

"Okay, okay," she whispered.

Reluctantly she crawled with me to the door, where we sat leaning our backs against it, facing away from the corridor.

"Are you absolutely positive that it was him?" she persisted. "You couldn't have seen him, Con. I mean, think about it logically. There is no reason for Hans Grunwald to be on *this* train unless he is looking for us. And he can't be looking for us *here* because no one in the world besides our parents, Uncle Aaron, Aunt Ruth, and Andrew Hart know we are here. And I don't really think any of them would have told him, so . . ."

"So . . ." I said, feeling my rear getting numb sitting there on the floor. "So I don't know how or why, but it was him. I'm almost positive, Hannah."

It did sound foolish. There was no way he could be here. It must have been the dim light, the night, the dream. . . . Everything seemed a little weird. I realized I was holding my breath and let it out with a sigh.

"You're probably right," I said finally. "There's no logical way it could have been him."

Nevertheless, we made sure the flimsy, torn curtain covered as much of the window as possible. And even Hannah kept her face hidden from the door for the rest of the night as we crossed over the mountains, through the tunnels, on the only route from the interior of Romania to its northernmost city.

◆

"Incoming!" I shouted as droplets released by screaming pigeons overhead exploded on Hannah's crisp navy blue backpack, landing with the accuracy of laser-guided missiles.

Bull's-eye.

"Yuk, yuk, yuk!" Hannah shrieked, trying to avoid any more payload from the flock still circling the "sky" of the Iasi train terminal's high glass ceiling.

"Don't stand there laughing, Con," she snapped. "Help me wipe it off."

"Yeah, sure," I said. "With what? By the way, they're coming back. Run, Hannah, the birds are after you!" Choking with laughter, I watched as the whole screaming herd turned toward us for another flyby.

She ran. Right into Aunt Ruth and Andrew Hart.

"Hi, Andy. How'd you get here before us?" I shook his hand while Aunt Ruth comforted Hannah—wiping off the bird droppings with a tissue and telling her over and over how sorry they were that Mr. Hart missed the train, and asking, without waiting for an answer, if everything had been quite comfortable and safe.

Neither, I thought but kept quiet.

"Sorry I missed you guys," Andrew Hart said. "It's a long story. But when I called the ambassador, he was none too pleased, as you can imagine. He insisted I catch a flight up to be here at your service during your holiday. So I rushed to the airport and caught the red-eye into Iasi."

Our so-called escort was about my height, but he had a wrestler's broad shoulders and thick neck. He was dressed in a sports coat, tie, and khaki pants—with creases. He had blue eyes behind round, wire-rimmed glasses, and I didn't much like the way he looked at Hannah—all smiles and can-I-be-of-service-young-lady attitude.

"Hope you weren't frightened, alone on the train like that in a strange country," he said to me as if I were some kind of kid.

"It's not that strange," I replied. "And there was nothing bigger than a mouse to be afraid of," I assured him while looking back at the train to see if Dirty Harry had been a dream or really was there.

"Ugh—a mouse, really?" Aunt Ruth greeted me with a warm hug. I had never met her before. She didn't look at all like a VIP's wife. She looked like a mom, with short, curly black hair, casual clothes, no makeup, and a great big friendly grin. I liked her at once.

And there was a limo.

"Cooool," I said, admiring the car.

A driver stood beside the black Mercedes-Benz. He was a jovial-looking fellow with a bushy brown mustache, a mop of hair to go with it, and the belly of a man who appeared to enjoy his food.

"This is our driver, Ovidiu."

"Call me Ovi," he said, making a little bow and holding the door open for us.

The sun was bright on the snow-covered ground. A rusty old tram rambled past, filled to overflowing with people on their way to work. The terrors of the night had disappeared along with the morning mist. I was embarrassed about my hysterics on the train and hoped Hannah would keep her mouth shut about my "sighting" of Hans Grunwald. There was no sign of him in the crowd still streaming from the station, so I told myself it had all been a bad nightmare.

"I need a hot shower," Hannah told her aunt.

"I need a hot meal," I said, feeling every bit the VIP as I slid across the smooth leather seats of the ambassador's limo.

"Please hurry, everyone," Ovi said in a thick Romanian accent. "Be happy, don't worry . . . but *do* hurry. More of those . . . those—how you say in English?—skinhead jugs are arriving from the train. Foreigners trying to make trouble. We must to go quickly."

"I think you mean skinhead *thugs*, Ovi," Andrew told him. "And yes, by all means hurry. We don't want trouble."

I couldn't have agreed more. And Ovi's pronouncement was more troublesome than he could have imagined. It meant Hans Grunwald did have a possible reason to be on that train. Fear crept back into my bones. All night I had told myself Hannah was right, that Grunwald couldn't possibly *know* we were on the train, so he couldn't possibly *be* on the train look-

THE BORDER

ing for us. But I had reasoned wrong. Old Nazis and young fascists were pouring into Iasi for the Antonescu ceremony, and Dirty Harry could be one of them.

"I need a hot shower," Hannah repeated, still embarrassed at wearing pigeon poop on her coat. She scooted across the seat, moving as far away as possible from Andy Hart.

"You okay, Con?" Hannah asked. "You don't look so good."

Get a grip, I told myself. *Won't do to have your fear showing*.

Hannah was explaining the pigeons once again to her aunt, seemingly oblivious to the implications of Ovi's announcement about the "skinhead jugs." Ovi was intent upon pulling the expensive car away from the train station parking lot and into the heavy flow of traffic as quickly as possible. Small, dull-colored Dacias filled the street. The Romanian-made cars looked like lawnmowers with cabs. Ovi expertly left them in the powerful Mercedes' dust.

"The smell is hardly noticeable," Andrew Hart assured Hannah, gazing a little too fondly in her direction. But I noticed him glancing back toward the train station, also, and took one last look myself—trying to put my fear to rest.

Aunt Ruth chattered on like a tour guide as Ovi drove, pointing out the sights of the city built on the foothills of the Carpathians. There were buildings dating back hundreds of years, and even older gold-turreted Orthodox churches with Turkish influence.

"That," Aunt Ruth explained, "is the cathedral. Iasi was the capital of Moldova and seat of the Romanian Orthodox church during the time of Stefan the Great." She glowed at Hannah, showing off Iasi as if it were her hometown.

As we passed the magnificent cathedral, bearded monks in long black robes and high pointed hats were making their way from the abby to worship, called by bells from a lofty tower.

In contrast, next to the beautiful cathedral with intricately

49

carved stonework was a plain, ugly apartment building made of rough gray cement. Clothes hung to dry along the tiny balconies had frozen stiff, looking like headless bodies floating in midair. Each miserable-looking apartment complex was exactly like the one next to it, most of them unfinished, with piles of broken cement blocks and mounds of rubble lying around the front doors. As far as I could see, rows and rows of the tall monstrosities covered what once must have been green rolling hills when Frau R. was a girl.

"Such a shame," Aunt Ruth said. "People reduced to living in these . . . these things. Did you see all the pretty little country houses from the train windows—the ones with the colorful painted designs? Everyone here would have lived like that before Ceausescu decided to destroy all individuality. He literally sent out bulldozers and leveled whole villages and towns so that everyone was forced into the same square feet of living space, in exactly the same kind of building. Awful, just awful what Communism brought to this poor country."

"Especially the cars," I added. "No wonder Communism failed, if those cars are the best they could do."

Ovi heartily agreed and added a few choice comments about his own miserable Dacia.

"Remind me to show you real cars," I told Ovi, thinking he would enjoy my *Road and Track* magazine.

"Wow!" Hannah and I exclaimed together as we came down a hill and around a corner into full view of a massive palace with marble columns, dozens of turrets, and hundreds of gabled windows. A huge bronze statue of a soldier on a horse stood guard.

"Now, that is no cement block." I whistled at the sight. "Is it the American embassy?"

Aunt Ruth laughed. Andrew thought I was serious.

"No, Con, this is the palace of Saint Stefan. That's him on the horse, too."

"Well, I didn't think it looked like Uncle Aaron—"

"Oh, I know about Stefan the Great," Hannah leaped in, cutting off my sarcastic response. "Stefan fought the Turkish invaders in the fifteenth century, right?"

"Good girl. You always did like history." Aunt Ruth beamed as Hannah went on to tell how after each victory King Stefan would shoot an arrow in the air, and on the spot where it landed he would build a monastery to thank God for the victory.

Andrew beamed at our little history star, too.

I tried not to gag.

"Pull over here, Ovi," Andrew said suddenly. "By the statue. And open the trunk, please."

Looking puzzled, Ovi did as Andrew said, bringing the car to a stop next to the statue.

"Here," Andrew said, taking Hannah's coat and putting his own around her shoulders. "I can see the smell is bothering you." He put her coat in the trunk and rejoined us in the car.

"Gallant Saint Andrew, the Not So Great!"

"Con . . ." Hannah growled, but Andrew didn't seem to notice me at all.

"I took care of the foul-smelling thing—" He stopped in midsentence, smiling at his own wit. "Foul . . . fowl, as in pigeon . . . Get it?"

Hannah and Aunt Ruth had the nerve to laugh.

"Do we have to have him around all week?" I mumbled.

"What was that about the week, dear?" Aunt Ruth asked politely.

"Uh, nothing. Just hoping we have snow all *week*," I replied. "Can't wait to hit the slopes. . . ." Hannah had heard me the first time and gave me a smug, happy look as she pulled the big coat around her, the perfectly warm car notwithstanding.

"By the way, Mr. Hart, how did you miss the train?" I asked. "Get *lost* in Budapest, did you?"

"Con!" Hannah snapped.

But Mr. Hart didn't notice my sarcasm, told me to call him Andy, and explained his delay in a sappy-friendly voice that only annoyed me more.

"I was late, and let me say again how sorry I am that I missed the train," he explained. "Budapest was one massive traffic jam, caused by farmers on strike protesting low agricultural prices. Anyway, bridges and roads were closed all over the city, on both sides of the river, in Buda and in Pest. There were tractors, horse-drawn carts, and demonstrators blocking the roads. They were even dumping beer off the bridges into the Danube River—"

"The Budapest Beer Party," I interrupted. "Sounds like the Boston Tea Party, only more interesting for the fish."

Hannah rolled her eyes at me and asked her gallant knight to go on. I watched, feeling a little like one of Hannah's sacrificial pawns.

A MESSAGE IN THE SNOW

THE UNOFFICIAL RESIDENCY OF THE AMERICAN AMBASSA-
dor in Iasi was not a palace. It wasn't bad, though. I got my
first glimpse of our holiday house as Ovi swung the big black
car through metal gates pulled open by a pair of snappy U.S.
Marines. The house was surrounded by a small courtyard and
hidden from the street by a stone wall. Old Glory flew above
the three-story redbrick building. Two more marines stood at
attention beside the front door. Very VIP-ish. Very cool.

"Thanks for the ride, Ovi," I said to our jolly driver. "I'll
call you when I need the car again."

"Okay," he said, smiling as if I could really order the car
myself. The man had a grin that affected his whole face.

"Don't worry, be happy! You understand? Nobody can't
do nothing wrong with you, not with Ovi around! Okay?"

"Okay. Be happy yourself." I laughed at his interesting
use of the English language, then taught him the American
version of a friendly greeting. He caught right on to the
slapped-palm routine. Before departing he gave Hannah a little half bow, kissed her hand as though she were some sort of
princess, and climbed back into the Mercedes smiling. Hannah blushed.

I liked Romanians already.

"Don't worry, be happy," I repeated to the marine guard

as I approached the door. But unlike Ovi, he didn't seem to appreciate my humor. And didn't return my smile.

"Hannah, darling girl!" a booming voice called down to us. "You and young Constantine come on up." Ambassador Goldberg was leaning out of an upstairs window. I followed Hannah, who ran through the wood-paneled front hall, up a carpeted staircase to the second floor, and into her uncle's big bear hug. He had a generous face with lots of cheek and a deep, commanding voice.

Aunt Ruth left us to take care of business in the kitchen, and I wandered off to explore the place, leaving the ambassador and Hannah alone so as not to intrude on the happy reunion.

High ceilings, small rooms, and heavy, ornate furnishings filled the three-story house. It could have been in my neighborhood in Vienna, and I felt right at home in the attic room assigned to me. I dropped my backpack on top of the fluffy eiderdown and went searching for the source of an enchanting aroma wafting its way through the house. I followed my nose—finely tuned to find freshly baked goodies—until I came to the source and found Aunt Ruth right where all good aunts should be: in the kitchen, taking care of business.

She was stooped down in front of the oven door, retrieving a pan of steaming hot sticky rolls, when I opened the door and discovered the object of my desire.

"Oh my," Aunt Ruth said, startled, narrowly avoiding disaster as the glorious pan of magnificent goo she was holding nearly slipped onto the floor. "You startled me, Con." But disaster was averted as she managed to right the pan and place it on the counter in one fell swoop.

"Did you find your room all right?" She patted me on the back with a still-hot oven mitt.

Aunt Ruth was tall and sturdy with a bright smile. My first impression of her at the train station had been right, I decided. Aunt Ruth would make a great mom. There was something very warm and honest in her face. And more important, it was clear that she could bake, as well.

"Con, it's so nice to have you here. Hannah has told me so much about you."

"The good stuff or the bad?" I asked absentmindedly, my eyes on her handiwork, hoping she would offer me a roll.

"Both, actually." She laughed. "Now, let's go find that darling girl. I'm sure she'll be wanting a shower after her close encounter with the pigeons."

I would rather have had a snack before going to find that darling girl, but I followed Aunt Ruth obediently out of the cozy kitchen. Away from the hot cinnamon rolls.

"Tell me more about the train ride," she said, taking the stairs two at a time, not pausing to listen to my answer as she charged toward the voices in the study.

◆

It was an hour later, after Hannah and I had both had a chance to shower off the train grit and had joined Aunt Ruth back in the kitchen, that she finally offered me one of the delicious rolls. And I finally got around to answering her question about the train ride. I left my Dirty Harry sighting out of the story, as I didn't want to confirm any crazy things Hannah might have said about me. I also didn't want Aunt Ruth to stop putting more sticky buns on my quickly emptying plate.

"Thanks," I said, leaning back in my chair, full at last. "I needed that."

Hannah kicked back, too. Wiping cinnamon off her face in a most contented way, she smiled at me. It said everything I was thinking: No school. No parents. No boring old Vienna. Only Uncle Aaron, Aunt Ruth, and their staff ready to meet our every need.

And the Carpathian Mountains were expected to get more

snow overnight, improving ski conditions for the week. What more could we want!

Snow did fall. All night long, big wet flakes settled gently on the Old City of Iasi, covering the gray, the dirt, and the poverty. Toward morning the wind came up and blew it into drifts, shutting the city down.

It was the wind that woke me, blowing a lone tree branch scratching back and forth across my window. As I lay there in a half-asleep, half-awake world and huddled under the warm eiderdown, the face of Hans Grunwald returned to haunt me. I knew the true source of the scratching sound, but it reminded me of the creaking of the boat anchored against the dock—of the sounds Hannah and I had listened to for hours while bound, gagged, and stuffed in the tiny head of a boat on Lake Zürich. Left by Dirty Harry, who had promised to return and "finish the job."

I pulled the eiderdown over my head.

It didn't, however, shut out the noise of the branch against the window. *Scraaatch*ing. *Creeeaaak*ing.

Moonlight was filtering through the heavily falling snow, making an eerie glow in the little room where I was sleeping. My head told me Grunwald couldn't possibly know where we were staying in Iasi, even if I *had* seen him on the train. The rest of me didn't seem to believe it. I shivered from cold and fear and tried to sleep.

But sleep didn't return.

Finally, giving up, I crawled out from under the warm feathers to turn on the light and check the time.

No light.

"Ow, oh, ahh, cold . . ." I stumbled around the room in cold bare feet on the hardwood floor. I flipped the light switch again.

Nothing.

"Oh great," I muttered to myself. "No electricity."

My window looked out over Primaverii Boulevard, a main thoroughfare. It led from the northern hills of Iasi down to the beautiful palace of Saint Stefan, with me about halfway between.

I unlatched the window and leaned out, looking up and down the wide street. There were no cars, no streetlights. I wondered how much of Iasi was without power.

The green digital screen on my watch read 4:08 A.M. But that was Vienna time, and I was too tired to remember if we had crossed into any new time zones. Still not sleepy, I pulled the eiderdown off the bed and wrapped myself in it. The feathers made a pillow as well as a blanket, and I sat and stared out at the swirling snow as it continued to fall, blown about by the wind. The old birch tree outside my window groaned under the weight of the snow, and its branch continued to scratch the pane.

I wished the electricity would return so I could turn on a light and read to drive away the thoughts filling my head of that moment on the train when I saw Dirty Harry sauntering past me, swaying with the movement of the train, hat down over his eyes, head cocked to the side. The scene kept running through my head like instant replay. Over and over.

"No," I told myself out loud. "Hans Grunwald could not possibly have been on the train to Iasi." I said it a few times for reassurance, and when I said the words aloud I almost convinced myself. Hannah was right.

Murder, I thought, dragging my mind away from the present and back to another stormy January near Iasi more than sixty years ago. The murder of Gabriel Levi. Hannah hadn't mentioned going to Barsa again, and I hoped she had forgotten Frau Rozstoski's request because I had no intention of ruining my holiday chasing after ghosts, even for Frau R.

Struggling with old ghosts and new, I didn't fall asleep again until nearly six A.M.

◆

"CONSTANTINE! Get up. I thought you wanted to ski today."

It was Uncle Aaron. And it was nearly ten o'clock.

"And you can skip the shower. There's no hot water. Electricity's off. Iasi is snowed in, shut down. Get a move on, boy."

I wondered what the hurry was if Iasi was shut down, but my stomach moved me to the kitchen, where I shared a cold breakfast with Uncle Aaron, Aunt Ruth, and Hannah. Then we prepared to go skiing. Not in the mountains as planned, but cross-country in the frozen, empty streets of Iasi.

Hannah still looked a little sleepy as we donned all our warmest skiwear and the borrowed cross-country skis. As we dressed she reminded her aunt and uncle several times that she had never been cross-country skiing and would probably collapse and have to be carried back.

"You'll be fine," the ambassador assured her. "How hard can it be? At least we shouldn't run into trees or fall down slopes. You came to ski. We're going to ski!"

The aggressive diplomat pushed off through the opened gates and called for us to follow. We waved to the cold marines standing by the gates and plowed into the empty street.

Tramlines were frozen and covered over, shutting down all mass transit. Snowdrifts made driving the little Dacias impossible, so we were alone. The only sound came from our skis sliding across the frozen snow and Uncle Aaron's calls of encouragement to Hannah, who lagged behind.

My legs were beginning to ache from the unbroken, hard-packed snowdrifts by the time Uncle Aaron finally stopped at Stefan's Palace.

"Grand, isn't it?" he said.

We leaned against the base of the fifteen-foot high bronze statue of Stefan on his horse. It *was* rather cool, actually. Especially in the snow, with no cars to ruin the image. It could have been the eighteenth century.

"How many rooms are there?" Hannah asked, staring in amazement at the turrets and gables that stretched almost as far as we could see in each direction.

"Nine hundred rooms, countless corridors, gardens, statues—the whole ball of wax. Everything Stefan could want as a monument to his greatness. In fact, when Nicolae Ceausescu had his palace built in Bucharest, he made sure it was bigger than this one," Uncle Aaron explained.

"Well, he got bigger, all right," Aunt Ruth said in disgust. "He also got ugly. You should see it, kids. Ceausescu demolished miles of interesting historic architecture in Bucharest and erected the ugliest building in Europe. And he built it while bleeding his country dry. The people were literally going hungry! Makes me sick just to think about it."

We sat for a while catching our breath—watching it freeze in front of us—and thinking our own private thoughts. The silence of the morning without cars whizzing around was broken only by noisy pigeons fighting over the best spot on the bronze mane of Stefan's horse. The birds shook their feathers to remove the still lightly falling snow, knocking each other about and disturbing our peace.

"Keep those birds away from me," Hannah complained, looking in vain for something to throw at them. "Let's go see the cathedral and Revolution Plaza."

"I've seen enough cathedrals to last a lifetime," I complained but followed as we set off again.

The plaza was lined with statues of old heroes standing majestically over the city. And beside them some not so majestic stuff from the Communist period. Ceausescu's eight-foot likeness had been torn down during the December Revolution in 1989, but the plaque remained, set in the concrete base. *Nicolae Ceausescu. Beloved by the Masses.*

Hated by the masses, more like, by the look of graffiti

scratched and drawn over the words.

"Monuments to stupidity," Uncle Aaron said disgustedly. All around us stood rusted steel girders of crumbling cement statues. The old Communist hammer and sickle had been painted over by the people who'd had to live under the hated regime it symbolized. There beside the old was a new, still-scaffolded obelisk.

"Here"—Uncle Aaron pointed to the new obelisk—"is what will be unveiled on Friday. There will be neo-Nazis, assorted anti-Semitic types, and weak-willed government officials on hand to dedicate this thing to honor a man who had thousands of Jewish people killed in this city alone on one day."

I felt Hannah tense beside me.

"Aaron, this isn't the time. The kids shouldn't have to think about it now."

Aaron Goldberg, Ambassador of the United States of America, stood in the snow in that ancient city with his ski pole pointed to the words carved in stone at the base of the obelisk, and ignoring his wife read the dedication aloud, his booming voice carrying over the plaza as though he were addressing a large audience gathered to hear his every word. There was no reply, however. No thundering crowds, as there would be on Friday, cheering for the long-dead Antonescu. Instead, the flowery praise written for a murderous dictator disappeared into the silent, snowy mist as we stood on that bloodied ground.

I watched the droop of Hannah's shoulders and wanted to reach out and comfort her, but I stood unable to move, knowing nothing I could say would change the past or ease the pain of it. It was her people—not mine—and every reminder of the Holocaust built a wall between us. A place in Hannah's life I couldn't go. Couldn't really understand.

It was she who finally broke the silence. She took her ski pole and drew a large Star of David in the snowdrift in front of the obelisk, placing her pole deep in the drift. Then she tugged off a glove, unzipped her coat, and pulled her necklace over her head. She tied the delicate chain to the leather strap on the ski pole. A spot of sunlight peeked through the clouds and struck the small gold mezuzah, scattering the reflected light onto the whiteness all around.

"That," she said, biting off her words, "is my monument for all the Jewish kids killed by their so-called valiant leader."

She stood back, shoulders squared, looking at her necklace and beloved mezuzah hanging on the ski pole buried in the snow.

"Hannah, you can't *leave* it there," Aunt Ruth said in a very subdued voice. "It's . . . much too valuable . . . to be lost like this."

"No, you are wrong, my dear," the ambassador disagreed in a firm, decisive voice, as if a negotiation had just been concluded. "It *is* valuable, and that makes Hannah's sacrifice of it the perfect memorial." I saw in his eyes not only love but a new respect for his "darling niece."

Ruth Goldberg glanced from her husband to Hannah, appearing both touched and disturbed.

"Oh, I hate this," she uttered miserably. "How can the government be so stupid? I can't believe they're actually going to go through with this unveiling ceremony even after your protest. Can't you stop it, Aaron?"

They'd had this conversation before, it seemed.

"You know I can't, Ruth. And besides, now that it is set, it will be most instructive to see what fascists, young and old, crawl out from under their rocks to demonstrate for the same anti-Semitic and Nationalistic ideals Antonescu used to murder the Jews. I would love to be standing here Friday—unofficially and unobserved, of course."

It was an opening too good to miss, and Hannah jumped in.

"Con and I will come. I'll take pictures for you and give

you all the proof you need about who shows up."

"Yes!" I chimed in quickly, surprised at Hannah's suggestion since she had told me on the train she didn't want to ever get close to any more skinheads.

And Aunt Ruth definitely didn't think it was such a great idea. "Absolutely not. Not under any circumstances will you two get anywhere near this place. Do you understand? Not when all those . . . those *criminals* are here. Tell the kids, Aaron."

Uncle Aaron didn't say anything for a long minute. When he spoke, it was less like an uncle and more like an ambassador.

"It would be very helpful to have Hannah use her skill as a photographer. And the kids would be safe enough. No one would think anything of a couple of tourist kids taking pictures. It's true there will be plenty of people who wouldn't want to be on record as attending—"

"Aaron, have you lost your mind?" Aunt Ruth cut in. "I don't want Hannah close to these thugs."

The ambassador considered his wife carefully, then continued to disagree.

"I wouldn't want her close, either, if I thought there was any chance of danger. Hanging around the edges of the event and taking a few pictures would not be dangerous. There will be government officials attending. It won't be a riot."

"Then let Ovidiu or Andrew Hart or someone on your staff do it."

We were getting cold while they argued. I looked at Hannah and she shrugged, giving me a stay-out-of-it-and-wait look.

"That's just the point, dear. The official position of my office is that we are boycotting this event. The Romanian government is already angry at my refusing to attend. It is causing a strain we don't need at this moment when Romania wants, and I think needs, to join NATO. It would really cause a ruckus if I sent someone from my staff to photograph participants. Sorry, but officially my hands are tied. Unofficially, however, my niece and her friend could be in the area and I could look at the pictures they take."

"Aaron Goldberg, you have lost your mind."

My heart was pounding with excitement at the idea of spying for the American government . . . for real. This was too good to miss.

"Your husband is right," I assured Aunt Ruth. "No one would suspect a couple of kids wandering around like tourists, taking pictures of the city. We would be very careful . . . and we have some experience, don't we, Hannah?"

Uncle Aaron looked amused. "Experience?"

"Yeah," Hannah agreed. "Con and I used to practice sleuthing around Vienna, perfecting the art of espionage in case we ever got a chance to use it. We would get on the trams, find some suspicious-looking person, then follow them till they noticed us."

"And we were good, I might add. We actually put it into practice in Zürich once." I didn't add that we had been caught.

"Stop it, all of you. This is not—*not*, I repeat—some game of pretend following innocent people around Vienna," Aunt Ruth sputtered as she turned around. "These people will be vicious, and I will not have Hannah exposed to them. Really, Aaron, what are you thinking? I'm cold, I've seen enough . . . and I'm going home." She dug in her poles and pushed off across Revolution Plaza.

"Last one back does the dishes," I shouted, passing her, taking the lead, and easily beating everyone else back to the house.

5

TIMES THEY ARE A-CHANGING

THE STAFF AT THE RESIDENCY HAD BUILT A ROARING FIRE in the kitchen fireplace and one in the sitting room, where we gathered to warm up after changing into dry clothes. Candles lit the rooms, but the hallways were dark and spooky.

"It's so beautiful," Hannah said when we met up for dinner. "Sorta romantic . . . I hope the electricity stays off."

"Ha," I said. "Romantic until you want a hot shower."

Actually, I agreed with her. It was as if we had returned to the days before electricity, to what Iasi must have been like when Frau R. was a girl. I could imagine Frau Rozstoski in a candle-lit house like this one, in Iasi with her parents to attend the theatre or opera perhaps. In the days when she knew Gabriel Levi the musician, not Gabriel the refugee. I wondered what she thought of him then. Since he came from a different social class, I figured she hadn't known him well, but she said she had heard him play in a music salon and talked to him a few times. The city must have been beautiful before the wars and the Communists and the pollution and rust and ruin. I tried to imagine Mia at Hannah's age.

"Con? Hello, you're staring at me." Hannah flashed her hand up and down in front of my eyes. I blinked and returned from the past to our rather nice present.

There was a pot of chili boiling on the open-hearth fireplace in the kitchen. Starved after all our exercise, we filled our bowls and returned to the sitting room. Hannah and I sat cross-legged on the floor in front of the fire. A maid brought in a tray filled with crackers, sliced cheese, and Cokes for everyone.

Coke, introduced to Romania only after the revolution, was a favorite drink now. It was cheap and available everywhere, which suited me fine. Uncle Aaron asked for a pot of coffee to follow. I was hoping for some Romanian dessert myself but didn't want to ask.

The chili was perfect for cold, hungry skiers. We tucked in, and by the time night fell the electricity had come back on. But we convinced Aunt Ruth to leave the lights off as we sat around the fire playing chess and talking.

I actually beat Hannah twice, which told me she wasn't concentrating. Aunt Ruth asked all about my summer in Wyoming and the movie star who tried to steal our family ranch. I drew out the spider episode a bit, and my none-too-faithful friend reminded her aunt and uncle that they should take all of my stories—especially ones she couldn't personally verify—with a grain of salt.

Hannah's adoring aunt and uncle ate up everything she said, enjoying and loving her so much it showed all over their faces. I knew they were thinking about but never mentioned the gold mezuzah she had left hanging on the ski pole in the snow—and loved her more for doing it.

Too bad they don't have children of their own, I thought. Hannah had told me on the train how much they wanted to adopt when they learned they couldn't have children. But diplomatic posts kept moving them, and it had just never worked out.

On the other hand, they now had time and energy to lavish on us.

Chilling out by the fire, I was dreaming of many more such holidays with the ambassador and his nice wife when a knock at the door ruined the moment and my mood.

A cheery Andrew Hart poked his nose into our late-night reverie. He smiled an especially warm smile in Hannah's direction and pretended to be reporting for work.

"Things are beginning to move again in the city, Mr. Ambassador. I just got my car dug out. Saw your candlelight and thought I would drop in to see if you needed any help. The electricity is back on, you know." He flipped the switch.

"Hey, turn that off!" we yelled, scaring the poor guy.

"Riding to our rescue a little late again, aren't you, Mr. Hart?"

"Connn . . ." Hannah growled.

"No, thank you very much, Andrew," the ambassador said. "We do not need anything tonight, and you may take the day off tomorrow, as well. Ovi is on call if I need the car. But I will want you first thing Friday morning—seven A.M."

Glad he wouldn't be around tomorrow, I breathed a sigh of relief until Hannah blew everything.

"Do you think Andrew could drive Con and me out to Barsa tomorrow, Uncle Aaron . . . since you don't need him for anything else?"

"Hannah!" I exclaimed, unable to believe my ears. "I thought we were going skiing tomorrow." I thought she had forgotten about Frau R.'s letter, and I certainly didn't want Andrew Hart driving us anywhere.

Baffled also by the request, Aunt Ruth wanted to know why on earth we would want to go to Barsa.

"Check out some local scenery for a friend," Hannah responded not completely truthfully, ignoring my protest.

What could I say? That I would rather ski than help out an old friend?

"Okay," I suggested, trying to wiggle out of having the "escort" with us. "We could put off skiing for a day, but how about we go on the bus? Ovi could give us directions, and we could explore the town without bothering Mr. Hart."

"Absolutely not," Aunt Ruth insisted, proving to be the hoverer I had suspected. "*If* you are going, you certainly should not go alone. Public transportation is not reliable. No, Andrew can drive you—show you the nice monasteries and help find whatever it is you are looking for."

"Glad to be of service," he said, looking smug—I thought—as he took his leave.

"Why'd you have to go and invite him?" I asked Hannah when the Goldbergs called it an evening and went off to bed.

"Because I didn't want to ride on some crummy bus, that's why. What is it with you and Andrew Hart, anyway? He's a nice man . . . and kinda cute."

"Yeah, right—a nice man who has a crush on you." I ignored her "kinda cute" comment. "Besides—"

"Constantine Kaye," she laughed, obviously amused by my reaction. Which was understandable, since we were only friends anyway and jealousy had never really occurred to either one of us before. "He's too old to be interested in me. I figure midtwenties at least. Whadd'ya think?"

"I think I wish you hadn't asked him to go with us. I think I wish you would forget the Frau R. thing. I think we came to ski."

Not amused—and a little confused at my own emotions—I climbed the stairs to my third-floor room. Hannah had used my full name. Though still unaccustomed to it—I had taken Nigel's last name only a few months ago—I found I liked it.

I crawled under the eiderdown, hoping to avoid bad dreams again about Grunwald wandering around Iasi somewhere with his skinhead buddies. I wondered if I should have told Uncle Aaron about seeing him on the train. But I knew if I did he wouldn't let us out of his sight, let alone go to the demonstration on Friday and take pictures for him. So I lay there trying to choose between being careful—acting like a weenie-moron-wimp—or having fun. And in the end, I decided to follow my natural instincts.

I knew it was childish and had proven dangerous once before, but I still wanted in my heart of hearts to actually be a spy. Even if only for a day. And going to the Antonescu ceremony and taking pictures for the ambassador—it was just too good to miss.

And I wasn't going to let Hannah down, not when I remembered the determined look on her face earlier today when she left her mezuzah in the snow, making a monument of her own. Even if Hans Grunwald was there to take part in the demonstration, he wasn't looking for us. I, on the other hand, would be looking out for him. Advantage mine.

Hoping my instincts were improving with age, I covered up my head and slept.

6

CASA DE COPII

"WE'RE GOING TO REGRET THIS," I SAID MISERABLY, HESI-
tating as the crowded tram began to move. "Aunt Ruth is
going to *kill* us."

"Get on!" Hannah screamed. "Or *I'm* going to kill you."
She was holding on to the doorframe of the crowded, rusty
old orange tram, reaching out to me with her free hand. At
the last possible second I grabbed it. She tugged. I jumped.
And landed in a sea of crabby people—who, after having
Wednesday off thanks to the storm, didn't look too happy
about slogging through the thawing city to get to work.

"I can't believe you almost let me get carried away alone
on this thing," Hannah shouted in my ear over the din of
noisy travelers. "Whose idea was it to take the tram, anyway?
We could be in the embassy Mercedes right now if *you* hadn't
told Andrew Hart to take a hike."

Trying to ignore her—since she had a point—I concentrated on the crumpled piece of paper clutched in my hand. It
was directions to the town of Barsa, which Ovi had written
out for me this morning as we left the residency.

"Okay, okay. Just help me watch for our stop. Bucharesti
Street."

Stuck between a large lady with bulging plastic bags in
front of me and a sharp elbow in my back, I tried to maneuver

for more breathing room while nearly gagging on the over-powering smell of cheap, sweet soap. But we were blocked on all sides with bodies stuffed tighter than tuna in a can.

"Tell me again why your uncle wasn't appointed ambassador of Switzerland or France or the Bahamas?"

"Oh please, Con. Stop complaining. You looked happy enough last night sitting by the fire being waited on by embassy staff. And I still can't believe you almost let me be carried away *alone* on this thing," she said. "What were you thinking?"

"I was thinking," I said, trying to avoid the elbow in my back, "that this whole trip is crazy and we should be skiing. Aunt Ruth is going to be very unhappy when she discovers we went 'exploring' alone and not in beautiful downtown Iasi. You lied to your nice aunt."

People were beginning to stare at us as we carried on with what was our standard way of discussing things. I raised my voice; Hannah waved her arms.

"I did not lie. I implied. And I wouldn't have had to do that if you hadn't insisted on going without Andrew. But look, we agreed . . . you would go to Livada de Meri with me if I agreed to ditch Hart. That's the deal. We agreed, and we're on our way. So let's drop it, okay?"

I really hated it when she was right. But when she was right, she was right. And she was right, so I dropped it.

Hannah's black woolen cap was pulled over her hair and down to her eyebrows. In an effort to blend in, she had layered a couple of sweaters and a huge sweat shirt rather than wear her very cool-looking ski jacket. I had borrowed an old black coat from a closet in the servants' quarters. Looking around the tram, I realized our efforts to "blend" had failed miserably.

We still looked like foreigners. Lumpy foreigners with bad taste.

"Looks like you've had a few too many cinnamon rolls,"

I said over the screech of hot metal wheels on the frozen metal tracks.

"Ha!" She stuck her tongue out at me. "You look like a poster boy for the Salvation Army."

Hannah loved a good adventure, and she had convinced me that looking for Gabriel Levi's son would be fun as well as the "right" thing to do for my old friend Mia. My idea of a good time was not taking a crowded, smelly tram and then a bus twenty kilometers out to some old town, trying to find a broken-down estate—and a man most likely long dead.

"Livada de Meri," Hannah said with a faraway look in her eyes, rolling the name off her tongue like it was some kind of exotic chocolate instead of a pile of rubble.

"Just think, Con, we are going to see it today. We are going back for her. It's so exciting I can hardly stand it."

"Yeah, I can hardly stand it, too."

Hannah had her new Canon AE–1 hung around her neck, with backup rolls of film in her jacket. I had snacks in my backpack.

"Explain to me again *why* we have to do this," I said over the noise and commotion of the crowded tram.

Hannah has this low growl that she makes from back in her throat somewhere. Along with the growl she gave me, the I-am-woman-I-am-superior look told the whole tram what she thought.

"You have no soul, you know that, don't you, Con? No soul at all. We are about to visit the scene of a mystery that is part fairy tale and part love story: A pampered, rich princess turns out to be tough and smart and . . . and a real hero. She learns to run the family business as well as or better than any man, instead of sitting around waiting for a husband. Then she risks her life to save Gabriel Levi, who in turn gives his life trying to save her. And I for one would rather see the scene of all that real-life romance and bravery and history than all the sights in Iasi. Or go skiing."

"Who said anything about romance?" I shot back. "Her letter did not mention romance. And here's our stop."

A general surge forward propelled us off with the crowd. Dodging the miserable excuse for a car that nearly hit us, we made our way out of the crush of people that had moved like a tide off the tram.

Glad to be out of the mob—and able to talk without people staring at us—we progressed slowly down the hill toward the bus stop on the corner of Primaverii and Bucharesti streets, following Ovi's written instructions.

After I had called Andrew Hart this morning and told him we didn't need a "chaperone" after all, Ovi had conveniently turned up at the residency. Happy to help, he had written clear directions by tram and bus to the town of Barsa. Then, according to my description of its location, he wrote directions to where Livada de Meri must have been. On the foothills out of town, overlooking the river, by the bridge border crossing. Directions we sincerely hoped the taxi driver would understand. I was quite sure we were on a wild-goose chase. But I couldn't think of anyone I would rather chase geese with than Hannah. She was more fun than anybody else I knew. And I was used to hanging out with girls, since every summer of my life had been spent at the ranch in Wyoming with my six girl cousins.

"Did Frau Rozstoski ever marry?" Hannah brushed snow off a bench at the bus stop, and we sat down to await the nine A.M. bus. A white signpost in the shape of an arrow pointed north and said *Ukraine and Moldova*.

"No, she never married," I conceded, wondering what that proved.

"Well," Hannah explained, looking at me like I wasn't very bright, "she never got married because she loved Gabriel Levi."

Hannah let me think about that obvious fact for a moment before further enlightening me: "Every time I read the letter, it becomes more and more clear. He was married, so Mia never could have told him her feelings. She wouldn't have. And maybe he didn't know. Men can be dense. But he must have cared for her, too. I mean, he died trying to save her life."

I thought about explaining to my good friend that his actions simply showed an ordinary male characteristic: bravery. Somehow I didn't think she would buy it. Not with that dreamy, faraway look on her face as she imagined her idealistic scenario. And while I didn't want to admit it, I thought she might be right. I had heard Frau R. tell stories of her friend Gabriel and had seen her face as she did so.

"And *we* are going to find out what happened to Gabriel's son for her . . . before she dies." Hannah pounded her fist into her palm. "Don't you want to find out the end of the story that started on that terrible day in 1942? Just think of it, Con—we might even find the book. Can you imagine how much fun it would be to take Mia's book back to her?!"

I groaned at her female logic but knew that Hannah was determined to find Gabriel Levi's son. I just hoped he was ready for a visit from two American kids.

"You are whacko, Hannah," I said, thinking that despite her best efforts otherwise she still looked like a very cute American girl on a ski holiday.

"And you have no soul, Con. You are basically a very tall—not bad looking—walking stomach."

I wondered if "not bad looking" was better or worse than "kinda cute" but didn't ask.

"Okay," I said, "let me see if I've got this right. We find the place, take a picture of the rubble, ask a few people—in perfect Romanian, of course—if they know where we can find Gabriel Levi. Oh, and pay a visit to Andrei Popa, who should be easy to find. Just drop in to the home for old Iron Guard soldiers and ask him if we can have the book back. And tomorrow we return from la-la land and go skiing, right?"

"Umm . . ." Hannah nodded. "Yeah, that about covers it."

Andrei Popa had killed Gabriel Levi in cold blood and taken the book. I would like to find him, too. Hannah could keep the romantic stuff. It was hard for me to imagine Frau R. as young and in love. But it would be very cool to confront Andrei Popa face-to-face. He might find it a nasty surprise to hear the woman he arrested that day was still alive and willing to testify against him for murder. Maybe this would be more fun than skiing after all.

An old Dacia rumbled to a halt next to us while we waited. A woman rolled down the window and leaned out, jabbering excitedly in Romanian—probably asking for directions.

We could only shrug and explain in English and German our inability to speak Romanian.

It wasn't that helpful, and finally the frustrated driver shoved it in gear and the little car sputtered away in a cloud of smelly exhaust.

"Stupid Communists—forcing people to drive cars like that," I muttered. "The people should start a revolution."

"They did, dummy," Hannah reminded me. "December 1989, remember? Ceausescu and his wife were shot on Christmas Day. Hello? Where have you been, Con?"

And with that historical footnote the bus came. An old white, snub-nosed tub with rust showing through at all her seams, the bus was no more uncomfortable and slightly less crowded than the tram. No one seemed to notice us as we boarded. Maybe we were blending in after all.

There was a gypsy family taking up several seats in the rear—men, women, and children. Dashing men with heavy mustaches and wearing black felt hats sat smoking together at the back while women in bright red scarves and scruffy but cute kids filled several rows in front of them. Remembering our experience on the train, Hannah and I chose the front.

"We should have had Ovi drive us," I said after half an hour of bouncing up and down on the hard seat over a road with holes the size of bomb craters. "I think they built this bus before shocks were invented."

"We *could* have had Andrew Hart drive us, but let's not start that again. Here, have a Snickers bar and shut up already. Ovi can't just take us around, ya know. He's paid by the American embassy to drive my aunt and uncle, not their visiting relatives. And besides," she went on, "it's better this way. No one is going to talk to someone who gets out of a big black Mercedes. Romanians are still very frightened of authority, and ordinary people do not drive expensive foreign cars. Especially people in the villages."

"And you know that because . . ."

"Because Uncle Aaron told me," she said smugly. "And he ought to know."

We rode along in silence for a while. I studied my Romanian phrase book and looked out the window. The weather had turned unseasonably warm, and rivulets of melting snow ran across the road, making the trip slower than usual. The Communist dictator had not managed to destroy the countryside as he had the cities, and individual farm homes dotted the hillside, brightly colored with traditional designs on each house. Hannah kept oohing and ahhing over the "cute" farms.

But when the bus came near enough for the "cute" little houses to be seen up close, it was clear that while these homes might have escaped the Communists' bulldozers, the people hadn't missed out on the poverty. Every farm had an outside toilet, sometimes painted to match the house, and a horse and cart instead of a Dacia. I shuddered at the thought of being too poor to buy even a Communist car.

"Not much has changed in fifty years, has it?" Hannah observed, then proceeded to take out Mia's letter and reread it again, now able to recite it word for word. She was "taking care of it" for me. Like I would lose it or something.

.I went back to my phrase book. Mom thinks I am good at languages and gave it to me before I left Vienna. She assured me I could pick up Romanian because of its similarity to Latin, thus justifying all the hours she had forced me to spend conjugating dead verbs during my childhood.

Thinking about Mom made me realize how pleased she would be to know we were going to look for Frau R.'s house and how much fun it would be to show her pictures of Livada de Meri—if we ever found it.

"It's a mitzvah my mom would be proud of," I admitted to Hannah. "Just make sure you get lots of pictures."

Hannah patted her camera, which was concealed under several layers of clothing. Ovi had warned her not to wear it where it could be seen on the tram or bus.

It was midmorning when the bus arrived in the outskirts of town, and I was armed and ready with my Romanian phrases. I could now say, "What is it?" "Where is it?" "How much does it cost?" and "How do you get to the bathroom?" I was working on "Did you murder Gabriel Levi and steal his cool book with the picture painted on the side?"

There, just as Ovi had said, was a row of taxis. We got off the bus and took the one first in line.

Factories sitting empty, belching smokestacks, miles of unfinished cement-block apartments with rusted iron poking out of them, and dull-colored cars welcomed us to the town of Barsa.

"Ugh" was Hannah's only comment.

The cabby took Ovi's directions, which were handwritten in Romanian.

"This is like being in New York," Hannah the New Yorker whispered to me. "The cab drivers don't speak English there, either."

"Da, da," he said. "Casa de copii. Da." He gave the piece

of paper back like it insulted his intelligence to need directions to such a well-known place.

"So what do you think?" Hannah asked, holding on as the driver lurched into traffic. "Is this a good sign that he said yes—yes like he knows where to go? Or do we look like dumb tourists he's happy to take for a ride?"

"I don't have a clue. You're the one who thinks Livada de Meri will still be standing in all its former glory."

The driver sped along through the narrow, partially paved roads of Barsa, honking at any man or animal that dared get in his way. He followed a road around the northern edge of the town, heading for the hills.

"Why is he driving so fast? Did you tell him to hurry?"

Everybody in Romania seemed to drive the same way—as fast as their vehicles would go. We clung to the side of the little car as the driver flew around corners, honked, swerved, weaved, and swore at all the other drivers doing the same. Horse-drawn carts plodded along in the middle of traffic, adding to the hairiness. As we continued to drive north, the carts outnumbered even the Dacias.

"Find it, don't grind it," I muttered to myself as the driver stripped a few gears looking for one low enough to pull us up a steep incline.

"What if this casa thing is something bad?" Hannah asked, ignoring my car talk. "Whatever happens, we can't let this guy dump us out here in the middle of nowhere, okay?"

"Casa is house or home, I think, so it must mean house of something or other. Which doesn't mean it's Mia's house. Livada de Meri is long gone, I'm telling you. He could be driving us anywhere. You don't really think finding her house is going to be as easy as getting in a taxi and saying, 'Livada de Meri, please'? I mean, these directions are a little vague: 'Travel north five kilometers, following the flow of the Prut River, past the Moldova border-crossing bridge to a castle surrounded by apple orchards.' The river is likely to be in the same place, but I'm telling you, Hannah, the house was probably destroyed during World War II. Things change in sixty years. Who knows what happened to it during the war or under the Communists afterward. And that was the last time she ever saw her home, so it is probably a 'casa de rubble' now."

Hannah made a face at me and went on gazing out of the window, expecting to drive up to the front door of Livada de Meri at any moment.

I shivered in the cold and hoped Hannah wouldn't be too disappointed when we failed to find the house, let alone Gabriel Levi's son. But despite my protests, I was getting excited, too. Especially when things began to look familiar to me. I had heard stories about this area my whole life, and I wanted to find Frau R.'s house as much as Hannah did.

As the taxi reached the crest of the hill it had labored to climb, we got a glimpse of the Prut River for the first time. Mia's river, the one she could see from her window.

"Moldova," the taxi driver said, pointing across the Prut River. He spat like it was a dirty word and made a rude hand gesture in the general direction of the border.

Hannah whispered, "That didn't seem to be a complimentary gesture."

"No," I laughed. "I don't think it was. But, Hannah, it *is* just like she described it."

I rolled the window down to get a better view. The Prut was nearly frozen over. Snow covered the foothills in front of us, and snow-capped peaks of the Carpathians stood out in the distance.

"I wish Mia could be here with us," I said, totally glad for the first time that Hannah had dragged me out here. I wanted to hug her for it.

She had taken off her woolen cap and was clutching it tensely, hands on her lap, camera out now, ready to capture this moment for Frau R. She leaned across me and snapped off a few shots. "Listen to the ice breaking up. It's kinda creepy."

The driver pulled to a jerky stop shortly after we passed an old two-lane bridge with a customs booth and armed border guards positioned at its entrance. I couldn't believe my eyes. The mountains, the river, the border crossing. I was almost afraid to look up to where the house should be. Afraid it would be gone.

"Casa de copii," the driver said, shaking his head sadly as he took the money I offered him.

"Wait here, please," I said, using one of the phrases I had memorized on the bus.

He shrugged his shoulders.

"Was that a yes?" Hannah asked nervously. "I didn't hear him say 'da.' I'm *not* walking back to town."

But I was no longer listening, because there across the street I saw it. Totally standing. Livada de Meri, home of Maria Rozstoski, was right where she had left it.

Hannah reached out and took my hand. "Oh, Con," she whispered.

We were stunned. The gate was gone. There were no big trees left to line the path up to the house from the road. But we stood transfixed, looking at the same snowy lane Mia would have known. I could imagine her in a horse-drawn sleigh with bells jingling, riding with her father home from the woods. Some scraggly apple trees were scattered around, all that remained of the once proud apple orchard.

As we got closer to the house, we could see holes from mortar shells in the stone facade, windows boarded over or broken, but it was without a doubt Mia's childhood home. It had withstood World War II while she was in prison in Bucharest. It had survived fifty years of Communism and the efforts of Ceausescu to wipe out all individuality by destroying private homes. I couldn't believe my eyes, and I couldn't wait to tell her. We had found Livada de Meri.

"Quick, get some pictures," I urged Hannah. "In case we get kicked off by the current owners."

The shutter of the Canon clicked while we walked.

"It looks kinda scary, doesn't it, Con? Unhappy . . ." she said, seeing it through the lens.

"Unhappy? How does a house look unhappy? That must be a girl thing. It doesn't look like it's had much care, that's for sure."

Both the east and west wings of the house stood intact, but the diamond-shaped windowpanes that had once stretched two stories high, giving the Rozstoski home its sweeping view of orchard and river, were gone. Sections had been covered with plywood, and the rest filled with grimy, flat plate glass.

The closer we got, the more I thought it might be a good idea that Mia wasn't with us. It would make her sad to see the house now. Hard to compare it with the beauty captured by the artist on the fore edge of her book, the way her father wanted her to remember it.

"Casa de something?" I mumbled under my breath as we walked. "House of what, I wonder."

The melting snow squished under our feet as we trod cautiously up the road to the front door.

"It's huge," Hannah said, still taking pictures. "Much bigger than I expected."

And then an unidentifiable noise from within the house sent a chill down my back. It came again louder, and this time I knew what it was: a scream.

Hannah dropped her camera. We turned to face each other and, with a sense of shared panic, asked each other without words whether this might be a good time to run.

But before we could decide, a battered, heavy wooden door swung open and a little boy ran toward us. Screaming.

"Hey," I said as he charged straight into me, knocking me

backward several steps, then clasping his arms around my legs like a limpet.

"Ajutor! Ajutor! Ma numesc Poppy. Ajutor!"

Tears ran down his cheeks, making streaks through the dirt. His eyes were big and round and pleading, his skinny little body felt like a bag of bones clinging to me, holding on for dear life.

"What should we do?" I looked over his head in desperation at Hannah, who didn't answer, for her eyes were fixed at some point behind me and her face was going very pale.

Pulling the crying boy with me, I moved to see what she was seeing, whatever was scaring her.

"Oh no!" I gasped. For there in the doorway were dozens of kids just like the one clinging to me. The place looked full of them, and suddenly I knew why.

"Copii," I said, hitting my head with the palm of my hand. "Stupid me. Copii means children. The taxi driver called this place casa de copii, house of children. It's an—"

"It's an orphanage," Hannah interrupted. "And here comes trouble." She moved protectively in front of the child as a charging angry woman emerged through the door, screaming and waving a cane in her hand.

I felt the grasp around my legs tighten.

"Help Poppy," the little voice said again, only this time in English. "Please help Poppy."

"Con?!" Hannah said. "Did you hear that?"

But before I could answer, trouble had arrived. She grabbed Poppy's arm and yanked him kicking and screaming off of me, yelling and waving her cane at us, driving us away from the door, shooing us down the path, all the while ranting in Romanian.

Stunned, I couldn't remember anything helpful from my Romanian phrase book. "Where is the bathroom?" didn't seem useful at the moment, so unable to ask anything or explain what we wanted, I was powerless to stop her. Back down the path she drove us, saying all kinds of things it was probably better we couldn't understand.

Livada de Meri was no longer a place of apples; now it was a place of children. A dark house for abandoned children.

"I'll be back," I called to the little boy whose eyes still held mine until he was pulled away from us and back toward the house, which now looked more like a prison than a palace.

"I promise I'll be back . . . Poppy."

Despite the angry words the furious woman continued to turn and hurl toward us, I felt a twinge of victory. Poppy had understood my promise and told me so with a crooked little grin on his tear-stained face. And he seemed to stop struggling and give in as he was led back into what was once the grand home of Count and Countess Rozstoski.

Unable to speak, we watched, stunned, until the big door closed and they were gone. Only then did we turn around and discover an empty spot on the road where our taxi should have been.

Alone on the remote, wooded hillside, which had seemed so exciting only a few minutes ago, we looked in vain for another house. Another car, tram, taxi—even a horse-drawn cart. But there were none in sight.

"Well, that was fun," I said sarcastically. "Any more bright ideas, Hannah?"

"Con . . ." she growled—that deep don't-mess-with-me growl back in her throat.

"Kidding," I said. "Just kidding. Come on, we better start walking."

And we did, slipping and sliding along the muddy road in silence for a long time until Hannah asked what I was also wondering myself.

"What on earth were you thinking when you promised you'd come back? You think you can rescue him, take him with you to Vienna, maybe? You big dummy." She whacked me on the back. "And he understood you. I don't know how, but that little guy understood some English. Now what are you going to do?"

I didn't answer because I didn't have a clue. But with each step I took away from the house of horror on the hill, I was more and more determined to find a way to return. I would keep my word—for whatever it was worth.

POPPY

IT WAS AN HOUR AFTER THE TAXI LEFT US IN THE LURCH, an hour of slogging through mud and melting snow, that we finally found a small café with hot food and a pay phone. Fortunately, Ovi answered at the ambassador's residency and cheerfully agreed to come to our aid.

While we waited for Ovi, we ordered the only recognizable things on the menu: French fries, goulash, and gallons of Coke. Ovi had changed Frau R.'s Austrian thousand-schilling note into Romanian lei for me, which with an exchange rate of 1,300 lei to the schilling made a wad of money big enough to choke a horse but buy next to nothing.

"Do you think Mia would approve of us wasting our 'research' money on food?" Hannah asked, wolfing down the last of her soggy French fries.

"Money," I had to remind my foolish friend, "is never wasted on food."

The goulash was good and hot, and I ordered a second bowl.

Warm now, our feet thawed out and our stomachs full, we waited for Ovi and went over our next move.

"So Ovi's okay with driving to Barsa to pick us up?" Hannah asked for the third time.

"Stop worrying. He's more than okay. He's his usual jolly

self. And your aunt and uncle were not home, so he didn't have to tell them where he was going."

I looked in my phrase book and figured out how to order hot chocolate, and before we finished it Ovi had arrived.

His broad, friendly face broke into a grin when he saw us. He apologized for the taxi driver who had left us stranded.

"I tell you, nobody can do something bad now when Ovi is here. Otherwise I cannot make such good promises. Sorry I took so long in arriving, but I have not the United States Mercedes, but my Dacia. You understand? It's okay?"

Ovi talked so fast and so funny we couldn't keep up.

Our new friend pulled up a chair at the small table, ordered a coffee, then asked us to explain what happened. Which we proceeded to do, taking turns and filling in what the other left out.

"It was very nice of you to come," Hannah assured him after we finished describing the morning. "We did find our friend's house, but it wasn't a very happy discovery. And Con here"—she punched me on the arm—"made a promise he can't keep."

Ovi looked at me, without the laughter in his eyes this time.

"You do not want to go in casa de copii. But tell me what the little boy say to you . . . if you remember."

"Oh, Con remembers." Hannah leaped in before I could respond. "I will give Con that. He has the most amazing memory in the world, and languages are so easy for him. It really is annoying. Anyway, tell Ovi what the little boy said."

Pleased at Hannah's compliment, I hoped I wouldn't blow it, but the words did come back and I could see the tear-stained face as I repeated his words:

" 'Ajutor! Ajutor! Ma numesc Poppy. Ajutor!' "

"That is easy," Ovi explained. "He say, 'Help me. My name is Poppy. Help Poppy.' But—" Ovi stopped and shook his finger at us—"do not go back . . . okay? Nobody can't do nothing for children in casa de copii. You understand?"

Hannah's eyes were tearing up. "Poor little Poppy. There could be hundreds of kids like him in that house; I could see kids running all over the place when the door opened. And the sounds . . . It was awful."

The usually animated face of Ovi was empty and flat as he explained a little bit about life in Romania before the revolution, when Nicolae Ceausescu and his wife, Elena, ruled the country with their dreaded secret police called the Securitate. He explained, stopping often to find the English word to describe the terrible times, how people were forced to inform on one another, even family members, and how people lived without electricity to cook or heat their homes. How they had to go without enough food to feed their families and were forced to leave their homes and live in the high-rise apartment blocks, sharing a kitchen and bathroom with total strangers. Families were forced to have at least five children to grow the country for "the Great Leader," as Ceausescu called himself. Ovi told us that everyone in Romania suffered while Nicolae and Elena lived like king and queen, a palace in every major city. And when people could not afford to feed their children, they were encouraged to leave them in orphanages to be raised by the state, future soldiers for the Great Leader.

Hannah's head rested on her hands as she listened, wiping away tears before they formed.

"Before the revolution nobody see in the orphanages," Ovi tried to explain. "And afterward when doors were open we were all ashamed. Big shame for Romania. . . . Children lived like animals. No school. No medicine. Not even knife and fork—only fingers to eat. And kept in beds all day."

He looked down at the table, unable to meet our eyes as he talked. We didn't know what to say.

"Please to forget today . . . and little boy. Go skiing tomorrow, okay. Nobody can do nothing for Poppy."

I listened, unable to imagine such an existence. I could see the faces of my own family as I stared at the table, trying to control my emotions. I thought of my own mother, who would do anything for me, who was always there for me. Of my new dad, Nigel, who loved me enough to make me his son. Of all my aunts and uncles and cousins at the ranch in Wyoming. Of my grandparents.

I thought of Mia's wonderful childhood at Livada de Meri, and it seemed so unfair compared to the poor kids living there now. Kids like Poppy, who had no one to stand up for him, take care of him, love him, and protect him from the lousy person we saw jerking him around today.

How could I ever tell Mia about Poppy and the others living in her once-beautiful house?

Hannah laid her hand over mine on the table, thinking the same things, I knew.

"Con, I'm sorry I made you come. I wish we'd stayed in Iasi today or gone skiing. It isn't romantic at all, and there isn't going to be a happy ending. It's horrible. Let's go home."

Hannah was right. It wasn't like we had planned. And all our grand plans to find Gabriel Levi's son or Andrei Popa were not going to happen. Still, that sad, dirty face haunted me. He had smiled when I said I'd be back. I had given him something to hope for.

It was quiet in the café. None of us spoke for several minutes—the dark cloud of knowledge now hovered over our holiday.

"Ovi," I said, "I'm going back. Will you help me?"

The words he understood, but the question confused him.

"But I tell you, Con, nobody can do nothing."

"Go back and do what?" practical Hannah inquired. "Ovi is right—there isn't anything we can do for him. Even if you see him again, you'll just feel worse. He'll feel worse. Give it up."

Not in the habit of caring much about strangers, I *was*

surprised by my feelings. But I was so mad at the unfairness of Poppy's life and that horrible woman who chased us off. I couldn't let someone like her stop me. No way.

Ovi looked from me to Hannah and back again, uncertain.

Thinking the matter was settled, Hannah started putting on her gloves and coat. "Come on, Con. Forget it. We'll ski tomorrow, and this will just be a bad memory."

"The young lady, she is right," Ovi agreed as he got up. "There isn't something you can do, Con. There isn't something any of us can do. The matron at the orphanage has big authority. No chance we can't not get past her."

Double negatives aside, I knew what he meant, but I wasn't ready to give up.

"Wait, please," I said, and they both sat back down reluctantly.

"Hannah, when we play chess, you always find a way to beat me. You keep thinking till my patience runs out, and then you sneak up on me and win. It couldn't possibly be that you are smarter, so it must be the patience thing. Waiting and plotting. Well, please help me now, help me think of a way. I've got to see Poppy. Maybe we could buy him something that would make his life a little easier. We could use the rest of Frau R.'s money. I have to go back like I promised. And besides"—I tried another tack—"you wanted to see inside Mia's house, see where Gabriel was shot and maybe even the view from her bedroom, where she watched . . . all that romantic stuff, remember? Come on, we can't give up now."

I was pulling out all the stops.

"Together we can think of a way to get inside the house," I went on. "See Poppy and have your look around."

The light finally went on behind her eyes. She couldn't resist the challenge, and I knew she couldn't forget Poppy, either. Hannah was in.

"Yeah," she said slowly, thoughtfully. "Maybe we could

get in and take a look. We need a rook or a bishop. Maybe even a queen . . . something powerful enough to get past the woman guarding the door."

Our Romanian friend looked more than a little confused now.

"And maybe," she went on, "with Ovi's help we can find a rook at least, if not a queen."

"Yesssss," I said, slamming my fist on the table. Hannah was, as I always knew, cool enough to be a guy. She pulled her travel chess set out of her backpack, ready to explain our strategy to Ovi.

His face lit up. "Okay, I play chess good. Will beat both of you . . . but you pick a funny time to play games."

Hannah proceeded to explain to our friend that we didn't intend to play a game on this board but out there, pointing up the hill to where Poppy and the other kids were imprisoned in the orphanage.

The people running the orphanage were the black pawns. Hannah held up the red queen.

"This, Ovi, is what we need. Someone powerful enough to get us past all these defenses."

Gradually he began to like the idea of helping us get past the woman guarding the door of the orphanage.

"We must to make a plan," he finally announced, ready to help out.

"That's the idea, Ovi. But we are . . . uh . . . sorta waiting on you for an idea, here."

"Pawns I know about," he said. "In Romania we are all the time pawns. But a rook, bishop, queen . . . Queen . . . of course." He slapped his hand to his forehead. "Wait here, please." He strode off toward the phone booth by the door, shouting back at us in his booming voice, "Okay, I understand. Don't worry, be happy! Maybe there is something Ovi can do about something."

We were left momentarily speechless at his enthusiastic response.

Hannah did mumble something about another of my crazy schemes as we watched him gesturing wildly while talking on the phone. But she took off her gloves, drained the dredges of chocolate from her cup, and waited—semipatiently—with me.

Ovi returned to the table looking smug and happy. "I have a plan, yes. My friend he brings us to the queen. Right here. You understand?"

We nodded yes, not understanding at all but glad to go along. Glad to wait for a friend of a friend of Ovi, who he promised us might get us past the orphanage matron. We ordered more hot chocolate, and while we waited Ovi told us about the bad old days under Ceausescu. He was a college student in Timisoara, he explained to us, when the revolution started. He was in the crowd as soldiers opened fire, killing hundreds of peaceful demonstrators.

His body language changed as he talked. The expressive, funny guy changed when he talked about the past. Now he kept his eyes downcast, not meeting ours.

"Before the revolution," he said, "we could not get much food, unless we grow food. I never taste a banana or orange until Ceausescu gone." He patted his now round stomach. "First time I eat banana, I tried with peel on."

He grinned at the memory but grew serious again.

"And we were afraid. Especially Christians. We get in big trouble when we go in the church."

"You must have been very brave," Hannah said.

"Oh no, don't say that. I was not brave. I lied to go to college. I told them I never go in church. . . . I lied. . . ."

"That's okay, Ovi. You only lied to Communists," Hannah reassured him.

"No. My friends, you understand, they didn't not lie about being Christian. It was only me."

"Well, I don't believe that for minute, Ovi. Besides, that's the past. Forget it."

Fortunately, before this conversation got even heavier, the friend of a friend arrived. My first impression was that this guy couldn't get us past his own grandmother, let alone into the casa de copii.

He shook Ovi's hand, nodding a greeting at the two of us before launching into a stream of Romanian we couldn't understand. The guy was a wimp. I watched in disappointment as the two of them talked. If this was Ovi's powerful weapon, we would never see the inside of Livada de Meri or Poppy ever again.

"A little on the short side, don't you think?" I whispered to Hannah. "And it would help if he could speak English."

"I will, if you pardon the southern accent," he said in perfect English. "Name's Matthew Henry. Born and raised in Kentucky."

"Oops," I said. "Sorry about the short remark."

"Not a problem," he replied, clearly not bothered in the least.

"Wow. What are you doing here? It's a long way from Kentucky, isn't it?" Hannah was as surprised as I was to find a fellow American in Barsa.

"Actually," he said, "I live in Iasi. But I do volunteer work in orphanages here two days a week—"

"You do what?" I was recalculating his usefulness at lightning speed.

"I work in orphanages, including the one you visited this morning."

Hannah and I sat with our mouths open (murdering the flies, as Nigel would have said).

"I have a little office in Speranta Church here in Barsa, which is how Ovi found me. He knows the pastor and had heard that we work in orphanages. So . . . tell me what I can do for you."

We explained about Poppy, not about our search for Gabriel Levi. No point in confusing the help.

"So," Hannah asked, "what do you think?"

"Well, for starters, I know Poppy."

Ovi beamed as if he had *created* Matthew Henry, not merely found him. I nearly dropped my cup of hot chocolate.

"Yes, I have known him for about four years, ever since I came to Romania, actually. Poppy had just been left in the orphanage when I arrived. About three years old, I guess. Poppy is very bright, and because he wasn't abandoned as a baby like so many of the kids, it makes it easier for him to learn. Those first years are critical in a child's mental development. And this makes him luckier than most abandoned kids who never have that early care. . . . Sorry, I'm getting technical here. But it is an important difference. When babies are never held, never cared for, part of their brain simply dies—it never develops—creating huge learning disabilities and behavioral problems. Anyway, that's not true for Poppy. He is very bright, and I've taught him and some of the other children English. It will help them later, maybe help them get jobs."

"Why do you think he was trying to run away this morning?" I asked.

"I don't know today, but he . . . well, when things get very bad, he tries to run away. Lots of kids do. If they make it, they end up on the streets sniffing glue. It's not a great alternative. But you can't blame them, can't expect them to know that."

I didn't blame Poppy; in fact, I wanted to help him run away. I knew, of course, it wasn't a very good plan. Run away to *where* seemed to be the problem.

"What do you do for the kids?" Hannah wanted to know. "Teaching them a little English doesn't seem to have helped Poppy much."

Fortunately, Matthew didn't get offended easily.

"I do what I can," he replied. "There are fifteen orphanages in and around Iasi—some worse, some better, than the one you saw this morning."

Worse didn't seem possible.

"Why do you do it?" Hannah asked, even more puzzled. "How can you stand seeing those poor little kids? And leaving them there?"

"Why is easier to explain," he said. "I go because it would be wrong not to. Jesus said to love our neighbor as much as we love ourselves, especially 'the least of these' in the world. These kids fit that category for me. My wife, Suzy, and I saw pictures of the orphanages right after the revolution in 1989. American TV cameras exposed the very dark holes these kids have been living in. One can't help the whole world, but this is the particular spot God has called us to. So here we are. And I would love to help you meet Poppy. It would make him very happy."

Ovi was leaning back in his chair, smiling from ear to ear.

"What do you say, Con? Do you think he's our man?" Hannah asked.

"I don't know. Do you have any better ideas, Ovi?" I played along with her. It had the desired effect. Momentarily. Then he laughed. He was quick, our Ovi, and quite proud of what his contact had turned up.

"How about tomorrow?" I asked when Matthew explained it was too late to go back today.

But before he could answer, Hannah reminded me that tomorrow was Friday and we would be "otherwise engaged," helping out Uncle Aaron.

"No problem," Matthew said, handing me a business card. "Here is my phone number in Iasi. Call me when you have time. Come meet my wife. I will help you keep your promise to Poppy."

Later, heading back to Iasi in Ovi's Dacia, I realized we hadn't asked one person about Gabriel Levi or Andrei Popa. Overwhelmed by our encounter with Poppy, we had forgotten everything else.

Oh well, I thought, *maybe Ovi has another friend of a friend who can help us with that mystery, too. Then we can get back to our holiday and onto the slopes*. I smiled at the thought and flexed my muscles in anticipation.

8

BLACKSHIRTS

Sparks were flying when I came down the next morning and not just in the fireplace.

Hannah and I had waited until Uncle Aaron and Aunt Ruth went to bed last night before discussing what we had found and what we had failed to find. Not certain how they would feel about us wandering around Barsa alone, we decided to keep quiet about our trip.

Discussing what to do next had kept us up most of the night. But the day's excitement had driven all worry about Hans Grunwald right out of my head, and I had slept like a log for the few hours before sunrise.

Bleary eyed and a little late, I stumbled into the middle of a diplomatic 'discussion' between the ambassador and his wife. Evidently it had been picking up steam for some time when I arrived, and the atmosphere was as charged as the *snap, crackle, pop* of burning logs punctuating the heated discussion.

"I won't have the children endangering their lives today in order to take pictures of a bunch of radicals so the American government can prove a point to the Romanian government," Aunt Ruth said as she attacked a pan of scrambled eggs.

Hannah gave me a weak smile and motioned me to the chair next to hers.

"Stay out of it," she whispered. "My aunt can be very excitable, but she'll get over it."

"First of all, Ruth, they're not children," Uncle Aaron said with some exasperation. "And they most certainly won't be endangering their lives! Enough of the dramatics already, dear."

"Dramatics? This is not dramatics. I *could* give you dramatics. This, however, is common sense, not something highly prized by the diplomatic corps, I realize. And you *are* acting like a diplomat, not an uncle," she stormed, placing a big plate of scrambled eggs on the table with such a thud it upset a basket of breakfast rolls, which went flying. I got two of the crispy goodies midway between table and floor.

"Good catch, Con. You a baseball player?" Uncle Aaron said, desperately trying to change the subject.

I grinned at Hannah's uncle—a pretty cool guy for an ambassador—and tucked into the hot eggs, hoping to stay out of the verbal line of fire.

"Young man," Uncle Aaron addressed me seriously now, "Hannah here has just told me she is still willing to go today and take pictures of the crowd at the Antonescu ceremony. Despite my wife's worry, I do not expect any trouble. There will be a number of high government officials attending with their security details to prevent things getting out of hand. Still, do you think you could make sure nothing happens to my favorite niece while she is performing this service for her country?"

"Yes, sir," I snapped, stifling a desire to stand up and salute, as well.

"Oy, oy!" Aunt Ruth exclaimed, shaking her head and rolling her eyes at her mate. "My husband the ambassador is a regular genius! Does the expression 'the blind leading the blind' mean anything to you?"

"I expect the two of you to use good judgment," Uncle Aaron went on, avoiding a direct reply to his wife. "Promise me that you will leave immediately if you feel the crowd is getting out of hand or that you are in any danger whatsoever. Can you think of any reason why the two of you shouldn't—"

"You are asking *these* two kids to use good judgment? I seem to remember them hanging around known terrorists in Zürich last year, *and* it nearly got them killed, I might add! And . . . and . . ." She sputtered in frustration. "You are asking it of this young man"—she pointed at me with a long wooden spoon, dripping bits of egg onto the floor—"who remained in the direct path of an angry black widow spider in order to get information to help his grandfather? You are asking *him* to use good judgment and protect our Hannah? Oh please, that is as flaky as these eggs."

Flattered at Aunt Ruth's image of my bravery, I still didn't want Uncle Aaron to get the wrong idea about my judgment, so I rushed to reassure him.

"The thing with the spider was nothing, and I *will* be very careful, sir. And, Aunt Ruth, you shouldn't worry so much. I have grown up since those childish stunts."

"Yeah," Hannah said dryly. "Amazing how he's grown."

"We're on the same side here, remember?" I whispered while kicking her under the table.

I momentarily wondered how mature Uncle Aaron would consider me for hiding the fact that I had good reason to believe Hans Grunwald was in town for today's demonstration. But I quickly rationalized my guilt over not telling him. Nothing was going to make me miss this opportunity. Real spying for the U.S. government! I couldn't wait to tell our friends back in Vienna and the cousins in Wyoming.

"Very careful," I assured them again. "You can count on it, Aunt Ruth. I promise to take good care of Hannah."

Hannah, in turn, made that low growly sound in the back of her throat, reminding me that she didn't need to be protected and didn't appreciate my macho promise to do so.

I smiled nervously.

"Careful?" Aunt Ruth snorted. "Con, you are a nice boy, but you wouldn't know *careful* if it jumped in your lap. And you"—she pointed the wooden spoon at her husband—"Aaron Goldberg, should be ashamed of yourself."

"Ruth, I have taken your fears into consideration. Really, I don't believe there is cause for concern, or I wouldn't let the kids go. And I have made, shall we say, arrangements. They will be quite safe. And this is important. We need proof to convince the Romanian government that a dangerous radical element and foreign agitators are behind this terrible day. If I can show 'unofficial' evidence of this—evidence not gathered by the U.S.—it could be very useful in bringing the Romanian government in line with acceptable behavior as a future NATO partner. I'm sorry, dear, but having Hannah and Con present and taking a few pictures is valuable to all of us who want to stamp out this kind of neo-Nazi activity. And that includes the international police. I know a very eager Interpol agent who would love to hightail it up here if we could identify anyone with a warrant out for their arrest."

I couldn't believe our good luck. He was serious. After all our pretend sleuthing in Vienna, this was the real thing. And the fire in Hannah's eyes matched her uncle's. Wild horses, or a sweet aunt, couldn't keep Hannah from going to the demonstration today.

"What exactly do you want us to do?" we more or less asked together.

"Act like a couple of kids. Tourists looking around. Keep taking pictures of the crowd, Hannah. And you look around, Con. Sometimes it's hard to get a sense of the big picture when you're looking through a camera lens. *Don't draw attention to yourselves*. And come back ASAP."

"What kind of 'arrangements' did you make for your

pawns in this crazy stunt?" Aunt Ruth demanded, her eyes snapping like sparks in the fire.

"Andrew Hart will be there all the time," he assured his wife. To us he said, "Far enough away from both of you not to draw attention, but watching all the same. In the unlikely event of trouble, he will step in."

"Ah, well, that makes me feel a lot better, then." Aunt Ruth threw up her arms in mock glee. "Dependable Andrew Hart will watch out for the children. Why didn't you tell me that in the first place?"

Trying not to laugh, or agree with her assessment of good-old-never-there-on-time Andy, I kept quiet.

"It wasn't Mr. Hart's fault he missed the train, Aunt Ruth," Hannah leaped in to defend him.

Defeated, at least for the moment, Aunt Ruth served the rest of the eggs without further protest. But her gaze, which rested on her husband, was not a fond one at that moment. Uncle Aaron wisely avoided further discussion by busying himself with papers from his briefcase.

"Pssst! Look at this note Ovi dropped off for us early this morning," Hannah said, passing me a folded piece of paper with our names scrawled on the outside.

Dear Con and Hannah:
   Matthew Henry would be much happy if you meet in his house this night. Please to call me with answer. I wait you a response. Your faithful servant, Ovidiu.

"You gotta love his English." I chuckled.

"Could we go out with Ovi later today to meet some of his friends?" Hannah asked, hoping to warm the atmosphere by changing the subject.

"Sure," Uncle Aaron replied. "I don't see why not. Ovi seems like a nice guy—good employee. It will do you good to meet some ordinary Romanians."

"If they live that long," Aunt Ruth added before exiting

the kitchen, obviously fed up with the lot of us.

"She's not a mother, but she has all the instincts," I said.

A sadness crept into the voice of Aaron Goldberg when he replied, "You are so right, Con. It makes her a little overprotective of Hannah. And of course her issues are not frivolous. If there is any hint of danger, you two get out of there."

We understood.

"Not to worry," he said, lightening his tone. "She'll be fine when you return safely this evening."

Uncle Aaron gave us some last-minute instructions and three rolls of film, reminding Hannah that if anything happened to her today his life wouldn't be worth living.

"Thanks for trusting us, Uncle Aaron. We won't let you down. And don't worry, we'll come back safely so you can say 'I told you so' to Aunt Ruth before we light the Sabbath candles tonight."

◆

Drifts of snow remained, blocking some of the small side streets, but Primaverii was clear all the way to Revolution Plaza. Hannah and I had dressed warm in our own ski jackets, happy to look like American tourists today. Hannah wore leather gloves instead of her big ski mittens so she could take pictures more or less all the time without freezing her hands. Her Canon hung around her neck. We were ready and pumped at the idea of finally spying for real.

Crowds had gathered in Revolution Plaza when we arrived. A four-piece band was playing annoying oompah-oompah patriotic-type songs. Two rows of chairs, roped off with red cord, stood ready for the official government delegation. The crowd looked like normal, ordinary Romanians to me. No skinheads in sight.

We walked casually past the podium, which was being fitted with a microphone. It stood about where Hannah had hung her mezuzah in the snow. She stopped and stared at the spot.

"I'm sorry you lost your necklace."

"I didn't lose it, Con. I used it. There's a difference, and I'm not sorry. At least someone here today—whoever found my mezuzah—knows there are Jewish people left in Iasi who haven't forgotten what that butcher Marshal Ion Antonescu did to us."

"Shh, Hannah. You are looking very fierce. We're not here to scare off the natives, remember?"

"Right." She forced a smile, ready to blend into the crowd as a harmless tourist.

Police were milling around in their olive green uniforms, with muzzled dogs on leashes and a Russian-made Kalishnikov rifle on every shoulder.

We moved back toward the edge of the crowd.

"Let's sit here and watch for a minute," Hannah said, squatting on the curb in front of a taxi stand. She swung her camera around from left to right, taking pictures of everything that moved.

"Doesn't look like Dirty Harry's kind of crowd, does it?" I mused aloud.

Hannah dropped her camera and turned to me. "You're not starting with that again, are you?" she said, sounding peeved. "Hans Grunwald wouldn't have any reason to be on that train. It was your overblown imagination. And if you're trying to scare me, it's not funny."

"Wouldn't have any reason to be on the train unless it was to come to this event," I countered, hoping she was right.

"Just because it's his kind of cause doesn't mean he would come halfway across Europe to attend. You need to relax."

So I tried. Still, I kept my eyes open and my back to a building.

Listening to badly played military music in the cold gets old fast.

"Do you think the band would take requests? If they play that oompah thing again I'm going to scream. I think I'll suggest something from U2."

"Oh no," she replied, alarmed. "No . . . no . . ."

"Calm down, I'm kidding."

"No, Con, it's not that. Look . . . look what's coming."

I looked in the direction of her long-range lens and saw a sea of black coming up the street. Men in black pants and matching jackets with military caps or black ski masks were moving like an army in formation, each carrying a placard proclaiming their hero. The sound of jackboots pounding the street with military precision sent terror to my heart before I could even see their faces. The wave of angry neo-Nazi storm troopers advanced toward us, threatening to overwhelm us, filling the street and stretching as far back as we could see.

Doing my duty for Aunt Ruth, I pulled Hannah off the curb, flat against the building, out of their direct path. We knew we should run, but Hannah kept snapping pictures. Each man thrust his portrait of Antonescu or Hitler up and down in front of him as he marched. Every placard was made the same—the fascist hero of choice blown up and framed with a black border. This was *not* a spontaneous demonstration. As row after row of marching fascists filled the plaza, the band got louder, the crowd joined in singing, and the songs became more militant. We could no longer see the government officials who had been escorted into the front rows. And their security detail was nowhere to be seen. Wondering desperately where Andrew Hart was, we pressed our backs against the grimy window of a closed store, hearts pounding. The man who had led the procession reached the podium and leaped up to the microphone. The bill of his cap was pulled down, touching his black-rimmed sunglasses and leaving very little of his face exposed. He shouted words I didn't know but clearly understood.

I could feel Hannah's whole body shaking, but her hands

looked steady on the camera, pointed and clicking.

"Way to go, Hannah," I encouraged despite my own fear.

"Are people staring at us?" she asked without stopping.

"Not yet."

That wasn't exactly true. Some of the thugs cast dirty looks our way as they moved into the plaza. As the men in black continued to arrive, the crowd got thicker, the space thinner. They pressed closer and closer to us. I could nearly reach out and touch one of them. These were Dirty Harry's kind of friends; this was his kind of event. I knew he could be the face behind any of the black ski masks. It scared me down to the bottom of my boots.

Revolution Plaza was centered on one of the many hills overlooking the city of Iasi. The monument—now with the scaffolding off—was perched on the precipice of the hill, reaching high into the polluted sky. A circle of shops formed three sides with a traffic roundabout in the middle. Small side streets led off it into the maze of the Old City. I was beginning to think about an exit, and our options were limited if we wanted to avoid moving through the crowd.

Out of film, Hannah reloaded her camera and motioned me to follow as she moved along the edge of the buildings in the circle to get off some shots from a different angle.

Just then a roar went up as the next speaker rose to the platform. Fists pumped the air and Nazi salutes were snapped. The speaker raised his arm in front of him and held it outright in a Nazi salute until the crowd quieted to hear his voice.

And in that quiet the sound of Hannah's camera shutter clicking away drew the attention of a man in front of us. He whirled, saw the offensive camera, and lunged. But his feet tangled and he tripped and fell. Swearing, he struggled to get up, and we realized we had waited too long. A second man seized the camera and jerked Hannah's head forward as he pulled the leather strap in an effort to get it off. The strap held, and she yelled in pain.

Without thinking I lunged.

As tall, if not as strong as Hannah's assailant, I swung for his middle with my fist. It hit muscle, hurting my hand. *Oh no*, I thought, panic seizing me. *What have we done?* More and more men turned to see what was happening. And none of them looked at all friendly.

The man I hit yelled, turned Hannah loose, and came at me.

"Go . . . on!" I gasped as he swung his placard my way, slicing me on the neck. I dropped to my knees. "Run, Hannah. . . . Run!"

As the man swung again, I grabbed the placard from my crouched position, flipped it around, and drove it into his stomach. He stumbled back swearing, tripping up the others momentarily and giving me enough time to scramble after Hannah, who had run for the first alleyway.

"Go . . . go . . . go!" I panted. "Keep going no matter what."

We were faster in our hiking boots than the jackbooted men chasing us, but we hadn't a clue where we were going as we dashed up the tiny passageway between buildings. Somehow we stumbled through a courtyard door, which I slammed closed behind us.

"Oh, Con." Hannah collapsed against me, crying in pain and panic. "What if they find us?"

"Shh." I put my arms around her and leaned back against the door, gasping for air and praying they wouldn't find us.

The sound of their boots stomping past our hiding place was bad enough, and then our hearts halted in midthud as someone stopped on the other side and rattled the door handle, which I had locked, and pounded on the gate. We didn't even exhale. I could feel the gate shaking. Surely whoever it was must have heard my heart trying to get out of my chest. *Don't let it give way,* I prayed silently, knowing what would happen if they found us here. Finally the rattling stopped and the heavy pounding of boots continued up the street.

We stayed there until the footsteps were gone. The cut on my neck began to hurt. The blood had dripped and now dried on Hannah's ski jacket. Still we stood not moving, Hannah's face buried against my chest. We waited until we were sure the men were not coming back. Then waited some more until we knew we couldn't wait any longer. Carefully, quietly, I opened the door. Its creak made us jump. But the coast seemed clear, so we stepped cautiously out onto the wet cobbled alleyway, unsure which way to head.

"Oh, Con," Hannah said, noticing the blood. "You're hurt." She ran her finger along the side of my neck where the sharp edge of the placard had cut into the skin. The blood had already thickened and was no longer flowing. "It doesn't look too deep. Does it hurt much? Oh dear, is Aunt Ruth going to kill us or what?"

I laughed. The fact that a howling mob out for our blood was camped in Revolution Plaza—through which lay our only known route home—was lost on Hannah, who could still worry about her aunt's reaction to a cut on my neck. "Finding our way back to Aunt Ruth is going to be the trick. We can't exactly go the way we—"

Before I could finish my sentence, a hand grabbed my elbow from behind. "Hold it," a low voice commanded.

Hannah's scream was stopped by a black glove over her mouth.

"Shh . . . it's me, Andrew. Don't scream."

Hannah didn't scream, but she did collapse in a heap on the ground. "Who said I was going to scream?" she asked once she had composed herself. "But you didn't need to sneak up from behind like that, you know. We've had a couple of frights already today," she complained weakly, sitting on a pile of brown snow.

"Sorry, Hannah," he said, looking as sorry as he sounded. "But get up and follow me. Quickly." He offered her his hand and a pull up. "You're not out of this yet."

He led us over and around unfinished construction material behind row after row of the ugly apartment blocks, past piles of building material and garbage covered by melting snow. We dodged speeding cars across busy streets and through smelly alleyways until we were ready to drop.

When Andrew finally paused, we were across the street from an old brick hotel, the Iasi Metropol.

"Let's phone from there and call out the marines," I suggested. "We could use a rescue about now."

"Yes, let's," Hannah agreed. "We need to call Uncle Aaron. Con's hurt."

Andrew looked at the cut on my neck, then at the hotel. He evidently decided I would live without immediate attention and shook his head. "I don't think so. There's always a chance some of the demonstrators are staying there. Con's not bleeding now. You can wait a little longer, right?"

Easy for him to say.

"Yeah sure, I can wait," I replied, a little annoyed. "But I thought since you were assigned to watch our backs that you'd have a plan. I mean, you do have a plan, don't you?"

"Leave him alone so he can think, Con."

"I didn't expect you to get into a brawl and have half the mob swarming all over Iasi looking for you." He sounded a little defensive. "And if you remember, there was to be no American presence, so I didn't exactly *bring* the marines. But never mind. It's only a little bit farther to the synagogue. We can go in there and call." He looked to Hannah—not to me—for a response.

"A synagogue doesn't sound like the best place to hide from a bunch of screaming neo-Nazis," I replied despite not being asked. Hannah didn't look too thrilled, either.

Andrew assured us it was perfect, and without much choice, we followed.

It was one short block to a very modest-looking gray

structure with a Star of David etched in stone under a single window over the front door. As a place to hide, it looked very exposed to me, sitting in the middle of an otherwise empty block. The only fence around it was a broken-down wire one that *might* have kept out a wandering cow. Maybe.

Not Nazis. No way.

"Wow." Hannah stared at the unimpressive structure. "I remember now. Uncle Aaron told me about the only synagogue in Iasi that survived the war. This must be it. They know the rabbi—a survivor."

"Fascinating. But couldn't we at least get inside to discuss this?" Looking over my shoulder, I was happy to see no one appeared to be following us—at the moment.

I charged ahead of Andrew and pounded on the locked wooden door of the synagogue. It was opened by a shriveled-up babushka holding a broom.

"We wish to speak with Rabbi Altar at once, please," Andrew said in Romanian, moving us quickly inside past the surprised woman.

She took one look at the blood on my neck and rushed off, calling to the rabbi.

"Here, Con, sit down. You're looking pale," Andrew suggested, then tried to explain why hiding in a synagogue was a good idea. "Rabbi Altar has met the ambassador and Mrs. Goldberg. He is so pleased that America has chosen a Jewish ambassador that he will certainly let us use his phone and wait inside until Ambassador Goldberg can send a car. I better go explain. Stay put."

Off he went after the scurrying woman.

Glad for once that Mr. Hart was around to sort things out, I dropped onto a bench under a rack for coats and shoes. There was a box of yarmulkes. I slipped one on, wanting to be respectful. Hannah sat next to me, still shaky.

"Did you lose the film?"

She reached in her outer pocket and smiled for an answer.

"Good girl, Hannah. We got those creeps on film at least," I said.

"Something they may not be too happy about," she replied, getting up and looking out the door to see if any blackshirts had come over the hill or around the corner.

It was at that moment that Andrew returned with a spry, gray-haired little man.

"Keep the door closed," Andrew snapped at Hannah, who realized her mistake and jumped back out of view.

The rabbi greeted us warmly, kissing the back of Hannah's hand in typical Romanian fashion.

His English was passable, and after looking at the cut on my neck, he bid us follow him along the dark, narrow passageway past the sanctuary, then up a set of stairs to his office.

The office had no windows and was overflowing with musty-smelling books. There was a single chair at the desk, and a space heater overheated the room, making me dizzy. The rabbi closed the door and listened to the rest of our story.

"Mr. Hart," he said when we finished, "you and the children are of course welcome to wait here while you try to telephone Ambassador Goldberg. But if you were followed . . . I mean, there are those in Iasi today who would like to get rid of the only synagogue they failed to destroy before."

That had been my point exactly. But one look from Hannah and I kept it to myself.

"I think I can safely assure you we were not followed, Rabbi," Andrew said diplomatically.

Rabbi Altar did not look safe or assured. "Perhaps you should hurry," he said. "Try again your telephone call." He offered Hannah the only chair in his small, overheated office and left us there to reach the ambassador.

We waited while Andrew tried and failed to get the phone to work.

I sat down on the floor, my head in my hands, and thought over what had happened. Rerunning my mental tape,

I tried to recall each face in the crowd, each blackshirt thug. No one I saw looked like Hans Grunwald, but then, most of them wore masks. So how could I be sure? The attack couldn't have been personal; I felt certain of that. Hannah's camera must have set the guy off and one thing had just led to another. The issue still remained, though, that if Grunwald was there, he was sure to have noticed the commotion and then noticed us. Was he indeed in Iasi? Had I really seen him on the train?

Like a buzzing in my brain, the same questions came over and over. The reruns were making my head ache. And I wasn't looking forward to explaining the day's events to the ambassador and Aunt Ruth. We hadn't exactly kept a low profile. *Rotten, rotten luck,* I thought miserably. We hadn't come off looking too professional in our first real spy job.

"You know what I'm thinking, Con?" Hannah poked me on the shoulder. "I'm thinking this is a lucky break."

Color had returned to her cheeks and that dangerous sparkle to her eyes.

"And I'm thinking you're crazy!"

"No, listen, this is important. This synagogue would have been here when Frau Rozstoski was a girl."

"Yeah, along with hundreds of other old buildings in this part of town. So your point is. . . ?"

Hannah was radiating excitement, which was pretty annoying at the moment, as I was still worrying about really important things—like living through the day.

"In case you've forgotten," I added to bring my friend down to earth, "Frau R. isn't Jewish and wouldn't have come here. So . . ."

"So, dummy, she wouldn't have come here, but Gabriel Levi and his family might have."

She let that sink in for a minute.

I did begin to see her point.

"And we could ask the rabbi if he remembers a family by

that name. Con, this is perfect. We couldn't have planned it better."

Hannah had picked up the scent of the hunt, and her romantic idea of finding Gabriel Levi's son for Frau Rozstoski had resurfaced in a flash.

"We found her house. Isn't that enough?" I asked, not wanting to spend any more time than necessary in a synagogue with a bunch of screaming Nazis somewhere outside looking for us. "It was a long time ago, and he'd be an old man now. Give it up."

"Give it a rest, Con. Since we are already here, I'm at least going to ask."

Hannah, who never gives up in chess or in life, went in search of Rabbi Altar. Knowing I would probably regret it, I followed, telling myself it was better than watching Andrew Hart fight with the Romanian phone system.

TOP SECRET

9

A NOT SO SAFE HOUSE

"THE IRON GUARD IS ALIVE AND WELL—IN EXILE AND HERE in Romania. And now they have gathered again in Iasi," the old rabbi said when we found him alone in an attic room over the synagogue sanctuary. He was looking out its only window, staring at the street below.

The window was round with a Star of David cut in the glass. It was the same window we had seen from outside, over the front door.

"I have been dreading this day," he said, his shoulders slumped forward, "the day they would come back."

We had brought this fear to his door, and I didn't want to bother him with our silly questions, but Hannah pulled on my sleeve as I turned to go.

A bare low-watt bulb hanging from the ceiling added little to the light coming in the window. I sneezed, recycling musty particles back into the stale air.

Rabbi Altar didn't seem to mind our presence or blame us for the danger that was clearly our fault. In fact, he began to show us his treasures. To him the room was much more than a dusty old attic. It was a place of memory, and he was the keeper of the flame.

The wooden floor creaked as we followed the rabbi around the room, looking at blurry black-and-white images in cheap frames, priceless evidence of what was and is no more.

Against the wall at the south end of the room, a wooden cabinet stood floor to ceiling, a combination lock on the door. Rabbi Altar bent down and flipped the knob quickly, right, left, then right again. The ornately carved door opened to reveal magnificent holy objects.

Hannah ran her finger lovingly over Hebrew letters sewn with gold thread on the blue cloth of an old Torah.

"Why do you leave them in here, hidden away where no one can use them?" she finally asked in a hushed voice.

A crow cawed loudly outside and soared near the window. Rabbi Altar watched the bird for a moment without speaking. But he had not forgotten Hannah's question, and when he answered it, I knew she regretted asking.

"Because, child, there are no people left to study them, no community left to live by their revealed truth. Only five hundred Jewish souls remain in Iasi, and most of us are old."

There in that private, shabby Holocaust museum—which would never be visited by dignitaries, hadn't been designed by a famous architect, and wasn't listed on any tourist brochure—we heard his words and grieved, for it was true. They were all gone. The school children, the old gossiping grannies sitting on the street, hopeful young couples strolling through the parks of Iasi—all murdered by the combined efforts of Antonescu and Hitler and the people who followed faithfully after them.

The room began to feel like a tomb.

"Let's go," I whispered to Hannah, but Rabbi Altar was speaking again.

"On one day alone," he said, "a day in June 1941 before Romania even entered the war, four thousand men, women, and children were killed by the Iron Guard here in Iasi. Not by an invading army, but by other Romanians. Synagogues were burned, and those of us unlucky enough to remain alive at the end of that day went into hiding. Most of us were found and sent to death camps. I myself . . .'"

Rabbi Altar stopped there, unable to tell us his own painful past. He looked again at the crows outside the window, screeching and diving at one another.

"To think I have lived all these years trying to tell myself that the past was past." He turned back to us. "I was wrong, wasn't I? Today you saw them, people gathered in the same plaza where people were killed, singing the old songs, honoring the man who directed the pogrom. It is as I said. The Iron Guard is still alive and well, sometimes hiding its anti-Semitism as anti-Communism, but still shouting the same racial hatred."

I felt the congealed blood on my neck where the placard had gashed it. Such a tiny wound, but the mob had meant to do worse. We had gotten away. I thought about all those who hadn't. . . . No one was ever made to pay. Now those murderers were being honored. Where was the justice?

Rabbi Altar walked over to a rickety desk, pulled a folder from the top drawer, and said, "Look at this. Last year Simon Wiesenthal told me he had submitted to the Canadian government a list of Iron Guard leaders now living in Hamilton, Ontario, where they hold camps to recruit young people into the movement. Mr. Wiesenthal asked me to identify one of these men—Nelu Zurloff."

Hannah and I looked over his shoulder at the face of a man in his twenties. He looked neither cruel nor kind. Just a soldier.

"Did you?" Hannah asked.

"Yes, I did identify him. He was an officer in charge of men burning synagogues during the June '41 pogrom. But it didn't make any difference. Was he, or any of them, arrested? Were they sent back to Romania from Canada to stand trial for their crimes? No. This same murderer was probably in the crowd you saw today. And afterward he will go home to Canada."

I thought about how Uncle Aaron wanted to show Interpol Hannah's pictures in case there were known war criminals in Iasi. If these men could be arrested before they left Romania, they could be tried in the country of their crimes without long extradition battles. I rubbed my neck again. It had been well worth the risk if only one man like Zurloff could be brought to justice, I decided.

"I know Simon Wiesenthal, too," I said. "I mean, I don't actually personally know him, but my mother does. She worked for him." I told him about my mom's close encounter with terrorists bent on stopping Wiesenthal's work. I didn't tell him that I thought the man responsible for the attack on Herr Wiesenthal was possibly in Iasi today, too.

"God be praised his life was spared again," Rabbi Altar said upon hearing the story. "Herr Wiesenthal is a brave man, but I wonder sometimes . . . what good does it do, his work? He brings evidence, but the Odessa spends big money to hire lawyers for the old Nazis. Governments get embarrassed and sweep their mistakes under the rug. Nothing happens. And it is a race against time, too. They are all old now. All of us are old now—victims and murderers."

"What school is this?" Hannah asked, peering at a row of graduation pictures on the wall.

"Those," he managed a weak smile, "are my fellow yeshiva schoolmates. This is the class of 1938." He then pointed to the others in the row. "Class of 1939. Class of 1940. And that skinny young man holding the 1939 class sign is me."

"Cool," Hannah said.

"So many rabbis for one city?" I asked.

"Oh no . . . certainly not," he replied. "I received a rabbinical degree, but many of my classmates were in the yeshiva not for a degree but only to study the Talmud. Many studied only for the joy of understanding the Torah. See this one?" He tapped on the glass. "He was a mathematician. This one was a mohel. He owned the best bakery in Iasi. And he, I think, was a musician. Oy, oy." He stroked his beard and rocked gently back and forth on his heels. "All of us together in life, so young and hopeful, so soon to enter the valley of the shadow of death together."

In her letter Frau Rozstoski had told about the old gate-keeper—who was really a rabbi—shot by the Iron Guard on the day he was going to circumcise the baby Gabriel Levi. *He might have studied here, too,* I thought. *Or he might have been one of Rabbi Altar's teachers.* But Mia hadn't told us the rabbi's name, so we couldn't ask. But there was one name we did know, and Hannah didn't wait any longer.

"Rabbi, do you remember a man by the name of Gabriel Levi? He would have been about your age, maybe in your class. He was a musician. We know he taught music at some academy here in Iasi. We know he escaped the massacre in June '41 and went into hiding on an estate in the town of Barsa. We really need to find his family." She took a deep gulp of air before going on. "Do you remember such a man, or anyone by the last name of Levi? It's so important to us to find his family."

For a moment Hannah's question hung in the cold, stale air of that musty room. I held my breath, thinking what his answer might mean to Frau Rozstoski. If Rabbi Altar knew Gabriel, then he might know whether his widow had lived through the war and returned to Iasi. For the very first time I thought Hannah's crazy idea that we could actually find the Levi family and what happened to Gabriel's son might be possible. If anyone in Romania could help us, it would be the keeper of the memories from that time and place. It would be Rabbi Altar.

Taking his time, the old man looked at each picture, running his finger along the rows of graduates, mumbling the name Gabriel Levi over and over as he did so. Hannah pinched my arm, and we waited not at all patiently while the rabbi searched his memory in the pictures.

"Yes," he said, his finger stopped on the glass by a tall man in the back row of the graduating class of 1940.

Hannah gasped—and pinched my arm harder.

"Ouch," I complained quietly.

"Yes . . ." Rabbi Altar nodded his head. "This man, he was a Levi, a common enough name, you understand. There were many Levi families, and I cannot recall his first name. Um . . . a musician, you say . . . Are you certain the Gabriel Levi you seek was an academic and a musician?"

We both nodded. Tense. Hopeful. The crows circled around again with their annoying cawing.

"No, I am sorry, then," he sighed. "This Levi was anything but a musician. Hands of a butcher, and slow-witted, if I recall. No, I am so sorry. I do not remember the man you seek. There are no Levi families now in Iasi, none that returned from the Shoah."

"Please, think again," Hannah pushed, desperate.

Aware of our disappointment, the rabbi stroked his beard as he gave it more thought. But he didn't remember Gabriel and was far too honorable to lie in order to please us. At that moment the kind old man was saved by a knock on the door.

Andrew Hart stuck his head in with welcome news: A car was on the way.

"Ambassador Goldberg asked me to thank you, Rabbi, for protecting Hannah and Con. And he wants me to assure you he will make every effort to get them out without drawing attention to the synagogue and putting you at risk. The ambassador is sending a Romanian driver in a Dacia. And you two"—he pointed at us—"be at the front door in five minutes, ready to jump into the car the moment it drives up."

Off he went to await the car, leaving us to say our goodbyes to the rabbi. We tried to keep the disappointment out of our voices as we thanked him for helping us and showing us his place of remembrance.

"Before you go," he said, "you must see one of the most

important pictures." He led us to the wall by the door, and there on the left was a large frame with a cracked glass covering six faded pictures of differing sizes, all black-and-white: four women and two men. A pretty unimpressive group. The people in the pictures did not seem to be alike in any way, and I wondered out of the thousands killed why these six individuals were so important.

"Your family?" Hannah finally asked, also confused.

"Oh my, no," he said, stroking his beard again. "None of these people are even Jewish. These are the 'righteous gentiles'—people who risked their lives to hide Jews. We do not forget. . . ."

"Six," I said, looking at what appeared to be a most ordinary group of people. "Only six people in the whole city?"

Rabbi Altar did not answer right away, and when he did, it was a cautious answer, filled with sadness, I thought. "I hope there were more" was all he said.

"Con, are you thinking what I'm thinking? Look quickly. Do you think any of these four women could be a young Frau R.?"

It had occurred to me at the same moment, and we plastered our faces up close, wiping the glass, staring at the old, dim representations of four brave women.

"Frau Maria Rozstoski? Do you know that name?" I asked as we heard Andrew Hart in the distance calling for us to get ourselves downstairs on the double.

"The Count Rozstoski—I have heard of him, of course. Everyone here knew of him. He was the most powerful landowner in Moldova before the first war, but I have never heard of Maria. Why do you look for her in this group? I would have known if the count's daughter was helping our people. No, you must be mistaken."

We didn't have time to answer. Besides, we didn't see a young Mia in that group, and with one more disappointment we gave up.

"It sounds interesting, these names you mention to me, Maria Rozstoski and Gabriel Levi. Come again someday and finish the story," he said with a little bow to me and another kiss on the hand for Hannah.

"That's what we're trying to do, but finishing the story isn't so easy," I muttered as we stumbled down the rickety stairs and back passage to the nervously waiting Andrew Hart just as Ovi and a marine in plain clothes opened the door and rushed us into the idling Dacia.

Everyone had taken our attack very seriously—even Ovi concentrated on driving without cracking jokes. The marine asked us to keep our heads down as we rushed through the streets. Ovi managed to squeeze a reasonable speed out of the car and delivered us back safely through the gates of the residency. We were whisked into the house in no time.

"Brace yourself, Con," Hannah warned. "Facing those demonstrators was nothing compared to the whirlwind we are about to face now."

But she was wrong. Aunt Ruth was so glad we were safe that she forgot to say "I told you so." Shocked at the blood on Hannah's jacket, she seemed relieved when we told her it was actually my blood, from the small cut on my neck.

Uncle Aaron was pale and looked more worried than Aunt Ruth.

"I am sorry. I shouldn't have sent you. My wife was right," he said more than once. "Are you both okay?"

It was kind of nice to have him fussing over us, especially since it resulted in something hot being ordered from the kitchen.

"Of course they're not okay, Aaron. Look at Con's neck. Call a doctor at once."

Uncle Aaron wasn't about to disagree with his wife this time, and despite my protest, a doctor was ordered and we went into the big, warm sitting room to await his visit.

The sweet spiced tea and ginger cookies tasted good. The

fuss everyone was making was not entirely a bad thing. The more we retold our encounter with the demonstrators, the better I felt about our escape. And I didn't mind much when Hannah made my fight sound even better than it was.

The whole place had come alive. What had been a quiet holiday house was now a hub of activity. Phones were ringing, the marines actually looked like they were guarding something, and secretaries had come out of the woodwork, snapping to at Uncle Aaron's command to take notes and bring him memos off the fax from Bucharest and Washington, D.C.

"Andrew, take Hannah's film," he barked. "And don't come back until you find somebody to develop it today. This whole city closes down over the weekend, so move. We can't wait until Monday. These people might slip away before then. I want to see who was at that rally today. Now more than ever."

"Is this all of it?" Andrew asked as Hannah dug in her pocket for the first two rolls and handed him the camera off the table.

She nodded. "The guy grabbed for my camera, but Con beat him off."

I glowed, and Aunt Ruth gasped. Again.

"Go," the ambassador commanded. "Call me when the film is developed. Day or night."

"Right, sir." Andrew looked at Hannah as he left. "I'm glad you kids are safe," he said. "Try to stay put for a while, okay?"

Uncle Aaron and Aunt Ruth agreed that going out again into the streets of Iasi was not an option. Instead of Ovi taking us to Matthew and Suzy Henry's home for dinner, Aunt Ruth insisted they come to the residency for a Sabbath meal.

◆

"Hello, Matthew." Hannah and I rushed out of the front door—one uneventful doctor's visit and several hours later—

to greet our guests as their car rolled to a stop. Not because we were so eager to see Matthew again, but to communicate a very important message before he entered the house. Surprised by our exuberant greeting, he introduced his wife, Suzy, who was looking a little overwhelmed herself at the sight of the old mansion, festively lit, and the U.S. Marines guarding the broad front door.

"Say," Hannah said quickly before her aunt and uncle joined us, "would you two mind not mentioning our little escapade to Barsa and our visit to Livada de Meri yesterday?"

Matthew started to ask why, but the ambassador appeared at the front door then and stepped out to welcome them. Light filled the ornate hallway behind him, exposing lavish furnishings. Suzy reached out for her husband's arm. "Oh dear," she said. "We're not exactly in the habit of dining with diplomats."

"Please don't say anything," I whispered. "We'll explain later."

They nodded in agreement, quickly distracted by the elegant setting as Aunt Ruth showed them a bit of Romanian history in the art and fine furniture that filled the house.

Hannah and I could only hope Matthew and Suzy got the message, as we did not want to explain our "unauthorized" trip to Barsa and plans to go back.

In the dining room a crisp white cloth covered a long table set with fine china and cut crystal. A few minutes before sunset, Aunt Ruth lit the candles to welcome the Sabbath.

"Blessed art Thou, O Lord our God, King of the Universe, who has sanctified us by thy commandments, and has commanded us to kindle the Sabbath lights," she said, looking very pretty and quite happy now that Hannah was safe and sound. "Welcome to you, O ministering angels, may your coming be in peace, may you bless us with peace. . . ."

The smells from the kitchen had been making me hungrier and hungrier, and I was tempted to break off a piece of the braided loaf of challah nearest my plate. Deep red wine sparkled in the candlelight as Uncle Aaron held his Romanian crystal goblet up and recited a traditional Sabbath prayer from Proverbs 31. It was a tribute to his wife and had a special meaning on this night:

" 'Strength and honour are her clothing. . . . She openeth her mouth with wisdom. . . . Her children arise up, and call her blessed; her husband also, and he praiseth her.' "

The Sabbath had arrived and with it peace. Tears glistened on Ruth Goldberg's face as she looked from husband to niece. I don't know if it was exhaustion from the day, the warm room, or the candlelight, but I felt a glow around that table. I looked at Hannah and her aunt, so alike with their dark hair and bright eyes set deep in clear, smooth skin. Intelligent, strong, and good.

"We are fulfilling another tradition tonight, as well, Con," Uncle Aaron explained to me, drawing my attention away from his beautiful niece. "It was the custom in eastern Europe to invite a stranger to your Sabbath meal. And so tonight we are glad to welcome Con, who is certainly no stranger but still not quite family, either . . . and our new friends Matthew and Suzy Henry. Welcome." He raised his glass to each of us.

The first course—mounds of mashed potatoes, roasted lamb, and all the crispy, braided bread I could eat—was followed by a rich Romanian sweet. Whimsically called "bird's milk pudding," the dessert looked like icebergs floating on a sea of creamy vanilla. Each "iceberg" was really a meringue sweetened with honey and boiled in milk, then topped with a sprinkle of cinnamon.

"Ahh, tradition," I said, patting my full stomach.

"Con, how is it that you eat so much and it never sticks to your bones?" Aunt Ruth asked after observing me put away more than my share of the dinner.

In the flickering candlelight over a second cup of coffee for the adults, Matthew and Suzy told everyone a little about why they came to Romania and the very sad state of the abandoned children hidden away in orphanages all over the country, thanks mostly to the former dictator.

"Basically Ceausescu was crazy," Uncle Aaron agreed with them. "He wasn't only a Marxist but a megalomaniac, as well—an evil one at that."

"And his evil is reaping a terrible harvest," Suzy Henry agreed. "We still see it every day in the sad faces of abandoned children."

Matthew's wife was even smaller than Matthew and not pretty, exactly, but the kind of person you wouldn't mind getting stuck next to on a train or plane. Her short brown hair was thick and rich and matched her kind brown eyes, framing a serious but friendly face.

"And the worst thing they did was force people to have at least five children. Then they kept the people so poor they couldn't feed their families and encouraged—actually *encouraged*—people to give their children to the state to raise."

I noticed Aunt Ruth's eyes tearing up as the Henrys went on to explain what life was like in the understaffed, underfunded state orphanages.

"The state promised people their children would be taken care of, and Ceausescu actually thought he was going to have a whole army of children raised to be loyal to him. A kind of Praetorian Guard. In reality the conditions were unspeakable."

"How terrible." Aunt Ruth wiped away tears. "How utterly sad for the country. For those poor children. I knew the problem existed, but I have never visited one of the orphanages. I don't think I could stand it. I would want to take a child home with me so much. . . ."

Uncle Aaron patted his wife's hand, then covered it with his own.

"After the revolution," Matthew went on, "when conditions were exposed to the world, we saw the pictures. Suzy and I hadn't been married very long, didn't have kids of our own, and we both just knew we had to help. Actually, things were worse than we had imagined. When we arrived in Iasi, many of the children lived little better than animals. All of their dignity, even their humanity, had been stolen from them."

"Things are much better now," Suzy assured the ambassador.

Hannah and I looked at each other across the table. What we saw at Livada de Meri was better? Poor little Poppy looking like a scarecrow and trying to run away from a screaming mad matron. This was better?

As if to read our minds, Matthew said, "Not good— things are not good yet by any means—but better."

"But what can you actually do for children in such a deficient system?" Uncle Aaron asked, not exactly skeptically but with some definite doubt showing.

Well, that was like asking me to talk about the Walker Ranch in Wyoming.

The Henrys leaped at the chance, sometimes starting the same sentence and more often than not finishing for the other. Their excitement and the joy they took in helping kids no one else wanted were evident.

"We can make their lives less horrible, for a start. Physical comforts, better clothes and food, pain-killers, vitamins, medical care—hundreds of people in the U.S. send us a little money each month, and we pour it into the lives of these kids. Some do get adopted—that is the best outcome, of course. And we help place some children in small group homes with loving caregivers. But most of the children will live out their childhoods in orphanages. When they turn sixteen the state opens the door and they are on their own. No skills, no education, no family to help them. It doesn't take much imagination to know what happens then. So Suzy and I are committed to helping those kids left behind. Helping them in ways that can change their lives.

"Since we are both teachers," Matthew continued, "we focus much of our time and resources on education. We have simple job training and even a computer room donated by the U.S. military from retired bases in Germany. A whole American military school has been transported to Iasi—"

"And is now used by Romanian orphans," Suzy finished for her husband.

"What kind of job training?" Hannah wanted to know.

"Everything from cooking to car mechanics to computers. But probably the most important thing we do is teach the kids who can learn some English. It's invaluable in helping them prepare for a job someday. Next to proficiency in their own language, they need English language skills in order to compete for jobs. It gives our kids a little edge, which they so desperately need."

I listened to the two of them, amazed at their excitement about such a hopeless situation. It did explain Poppy's speaking English, which hadn't helped him when the orphanage matron dragged him back into the house. I hated to think what had happened to him then.

Matthew Henry was a small man, but I figured he would be a match for the battle-ax watching the door at Poppy's orphanage. I couldn't wait to watch him get us past her.

Hannah and I had relaxed when we realized he wasn't going to give away our visit to Barsa.

"Some of the kids, those who were not abandoned at birth but had some kind of family experience before they entered the orphanage, develop more mentally and emotionally, and so we can actually make great strides with them. Nothing, of course, takes the place of a home and loving parents," Suzy explained.

"Aaron," Aunt Ruth said, a longing look on her face, "are you thinking what I'm thinking?"

"Maybe, Ruth. We can at least look into it," he said, a

catch in his voice, too. "But we must not bother the Henrys about it tonight. It's been a long day for all of us. And now you must excuse me. I have to make a few more calls to the State Department in Washington before the week ends."

And check up on Andrew Hart, I thought, who had not yet returned with Hannah's film.

"I'm going to the casa de copii in Barsa tomorrow morning. Would the two of you like to go with me?" Matthew asked as he helped his wife on with her coat at the door.

"Oh yes, please!" Hannah and I both jumped at the offer.

Aunt Ruth reminded Hannah that she had agreed to go to the synagogue with them in the morning for Sabbath service.

"It was kind of you to offer to take the kids," Aunt Ruth said to Matthew. "Although I am not sure I want them to see so much suffering. It's not like they can help. But it is your choice, Con. Go if you wish. It will give you something to do while we are at the synagogue."

Hannah was trapped between a rock and her aunt.

She couldn't very well refuse to go to the synagogue, but she wasn't at all happy about missing the chance to get inside Livada de Meri and meet Poppy again.

"How could you, Con?" she asked me later when the Henrys were gone and Aunt Ruth had joined her husband upstairs. "How could you agree to go without me? And Matthew said no cameras allowed inside, so you will have to remember every detail and tell me about the house."

"It's not my fault you can't go." I shrugged. "And we won't have that many chances to get inside. I promised Poppy, Hannah. . . . I have to go."

I really didn't like the idea of facing that place without her, but I couldn't admit that to her.

"Well, maybe you have to go," she agreed. "But don't you dare have any adventures without me."

"I promise. Besides, after today, I think we've had our share already."

10

INSIDE

ABOUT THE TIME MATTHEW TURNED HIS LITTLE FORD Escort off the dirt road and onto the long drive leading up to
Livada de Meri, I began to wish I had waited for Hannah. Or
not come at all. I had the meager bag of things I had brought
for Poppy, but my macho promise to come back seemed
pretty foolish as we got closer to the huge stone estate. What
good would my visit and a few books and clothes do for a boy
without a family, without any hope for a future? Why on earth
had I come?

Years of war and then neglect had robbed Mia's old home
of its former grandeur. The shell holes in the stone facade,
boarded-up windows, crumbling gardens, and muddy entrance made the place look more like Vlad the Impaler's castle
in Transylvania than Frau R.'s happy childhood home.

"Don't worry so much. You'll do fine," Matthew reassured me.

"You can smell fear, huh?"

He laughed. "Just the fact that you have come to visit
Poppy will mean a great deal to him. He doesn't expect you
to rescue him, you know."

But that was exactly what I wanted to do. How could I
leave that defenseless little kid in such a terrible place?

"What about the old bat that tackled him and chased us off? How do we get past her?"

Matthew raised an eyebrow at my description but didn't bother to correct it.

"Not to worry. The director knows me, and she likes the resources I bring. Frankly, it makes her look better, and in her own way she wants to help the children. Anyway, she owes me plenty of favors."

Mom's expression "There's more than one way to skin a cat" came to mind, and I figured Matthew Henry—despite his size—found most of them.

He pulled the car to a stop between two scraggly apple trees with skinny, bare branches sticking out in all directions. Very unlike the apple orchards cultivated by Count Rozstoski—and for which he had named his estate.

"Remember, Con, Poppy is bright. He speaks fairly good English, and you'll like him a lot. But there are three hundred and fifty kids from eight to sixteen living in . . . well, conditions you probably can't even imagine. Stay close to me until we get to the director's office. Do what I say and remember why you've come and you'll be fine. I'm proud of you for coming at all. In fact, I don't know many young people who could handle what you're about to see."

I wasn't sure I could handle it, and I was increasingly sorry my impulsive nature had me once again in hot water. And I wondered really in my heart of hearts why I *had* come. My promise to Poppy? A desire to defy the woman who had chased us off? Or simply wanting to see the scene of the crime in the grand foyer of Mia's house? Whatever my motives, they certainly weren't as pure as Matthew seemed to think.

This, however, didn't feel like the time to back out.

"Okay, let's go," I gulped.

"First we pray."

Matthew bowed his head then, right there in the Escort, and began praying in his soft southern drawl.

Oh boy. Now I've done it, I thought as he prayed for God to give us strength. *If someone who does this every day needs divine assistance, I'm in big trouble.*

"How do you stand to come all the time?" I inquired as we slogged through the mud up to the front door. A slow drizzle was falling from a gray sky. It was cold enough to be miserable, but not cold enough to snow and cover over the whole mess again. The smell of coal oil filled the air, burning my nose and making my eyes water.

"Because we see some progress," he answered me. "Believe it or not, things are much better than when we arrived a few years ago. And I have plans to keep improving not only their daily lives but also the long-term prospects for these kids." He stopped, his face thoughtful. "I don't know how to explain this to you, but I . . . well, I feel God's pleasure when I'm with the kids."

Okay, I thought, *you're right. I don't get it.* But ready or not, here I was, for at that moment the door was opened by a square-jawed, stocky woman who gave us no greeting. She had lavender-colored hair, teased and sprayed stiff, and was wearing a white medical jacket buttoned over a bulging middle, black stockings, and wooden clogs. With a mumbled response to Matthew's friendly greeting, she held the door open. My first reaction was *No wonder they don't allow cameras.*

My second reaction was to cover my nose. The smell of urine, sweat, and dirt mixed with long-spoiled food hit my stomach and made it churn. Trying not to lose my breakfast, I forced my eyes to focus on the kids. Kids all over the place. A small child with her hands tied together in her lap sat in a little chair, rocking back and forth against the wall, hitting her tiny head each time. No one noticed. No one stopped her. Big boys with shaved heads stood menacingly in a group by the old grand staircase; they were holding a smaller boy, who was struggling to get away. I was there in the vast hallway where Frau R.'s family would have welcomed their important guests. But instead of focusing on details of the room and where Gabriel's body might have lain, I reeled outside and lost the battle with my breakfast.

Regaining my composure before Matthew missed me, I stumbled back in to see him surrounded by a sea of kids, many taller than he was but all vying for his attention, their shaved heads bouncing up and down as they reached out to him. The hair job looked recent and like it was done by a butcher, not a barber. On every head were nicks and bumps, giving evidence that the razor had been quickly ripped across each skull without pattern or design. Loose-fitting, drab clothing hung off their thin frames. I covered my mouth and nose to shut out some of the odor and took deep breaths, determined to control my heaving stomach.

Leaning against the doorframe, I hoped the kids wouldn't notice me. My six-foot frame was hard to hide, however, and I stood out and over everyone there. Soon I was surrounded by big and little kids checking out the tall blond stranger. I was bombarded with tugs on my clothes, grasping hands, and begging voices I couldn't understand. My voice came out like a croak as I tried "Hello" in English, German, and even Romanian. My few tourist phrases in Romanian failed to come to me, but they wouldn't have been that useful anyway.

A very small child pushed between the bigger kids in the crowd around Matthew and tried to check out my pockets. Remembering the Jolly Rancher candy Suzy had given me for this moment, I pulled one out and placed it in the dirty little hands. Grateful, the small child wandered off, trying to unwrap the sweet. With shaved heads and everyone wearing similar clothes, I couldn't tell if it was a boy or girl. Worse than the smell, worse than the cold miserable place, I realized with a jolt of anger, these kids had all been robbed of their individuality, their dignity. They were nothing.

Except to Matthew.

Matthew took his time moving through the group, gently patting a little one on the top of the head, hugging a dark gypsy child who might have been a boy, scolding a bully who pushed a younger child aside. He stopped to read a crumpled piece of paper shoved into his hand and smiled his approval at the author. I watched him, amazed. He actually did look happy in the middle of that ragtag bunch of rabble. I decided if this was the best he could do for these kids, he might as well go back to Kentucky. I had never smelled poverty and despair. I didn't like it, and I wanted to run back to civilization at the residency.

But the gentle man kept smiling, and somehow we moved forward across the vast entryway, which had long since lost its black-and-white tile I remembered from Frau R.'s description. The broad staircase in front of me was as she had described it. Only, the woman standing at the top of the stairs staring down at us was no aristocrat. And no friend, either. The director of this madhouse had a stern face to match her white doctor's jacket. Not my idea of a mother figure for hundreds of motherless children.

Recognizing absolute authority, the kids melted away from us as we started up the old, scarred wooden stairs. I had the very familiar feeling of approaching the principal's office.

She stood, this director of the casa de copii, with her arms folded across her chest, high-heeled shoes planted solidly together at the edge of the first step, shoulders back. Her hair color appeared to have come out of the same bottle used by the woman who had opened the front door for us, but the similarity ended there. Authority was written all over Dr. Cornilia Lavinia.

"Ms. Gaul in the flesh," I muttered under my breath.

"Excuse me?" Matthew whispered back.

"Never mind. Frau Director just looks like the principal of my school, that's all."

Despite the bluish hair, green eye shadow, and pink lipstick, which proper Principal Gaul wouldn't have worn on a bet, I was staring at the same squinty-eyed, don't-even-think-about-messing-with-me look I had grown to know and hate back at the American International School in Vienna.

"Good afternoon, Dr. Lavinia. Let me introduce my friend Constantine Kaye. And for his benefit, I suggest we all speak German, a language shared by the three of us."

Dr. Lavinia didn't appear too concerned about my benefit, but her German was good and I was glad to be able to understand their conversation and not have to stand there like Balaam's donkey gone dumb again.

"The child in question will be brought here to my office shortly. You will be allowed forty-five minutes together."

Pronouncing it like a sentence for some criminal offense, she then inspected the bag of things I had brought for Poppy as though expecting to find a weapon.

"Thanks, Warden—I mean, Frau Director," I said as she handed it back.

Matthew shot me a warning glance to cool it, and I refrained from further comment as she pronounced the Redskins cap and sweat shirt acceptable gifts. "But you understand Poppy won't be able to keep these things long, don't you?" she added.

Matthew looked uncomfortable but gave a resigned shrug and agreed. "I understand."

"Well, I don't," I snapped. "You mean I've taken the trouble to come here to give a little boy a few things he desperately needs, and you're telling me he won't be allowed to keep them? Why not?"

I knew at once that I had gone too far. Dr. Lavinia wasn't used to "children" speaking back to her. Sensing my mistake, I smiled weakly and backtracked: "Please . . . that is, explain why . . . why he cannot keep them. . . ."

It was Matthew who explained and saved me from my ramblings. "None of the children have a place for personal things, Con. But never mind. He will wear them one day and be king. It's the fact that you are interested in him that matters."

Dr. Lavinia chose to ignore my insolence, or stored it up for later use, I wasn't sure. At any rate, she did not feel compelled to share with me why the children in her care could not have anything of their very own. Not one single private treasure, not even a piece of clothing to call their own.

"So," the director said, the details settled, "I am going now. You wait here. Do not touch anything. And remember, you will have only forty-five minutes with the boy."

Like Poppy had such a busy schedule being herded from one room to another.

"I'm off, too," Matthew said, to my surprise. "But don't worry, Dr. Lavinia. Constantine will be fine here alone. I have a computer class for the older boys now. In fact, I'm late. Enjoy Poppy. And by the way, Poppy is my nickname for him; his last name is Popa."

The two of them left and I was alone in a room at Livada de Meri. Terrified, I waited, wondering what I was going to say to the little boy I had seen all of three minutes. Wondering what he would expect from me.

I should be on the slopes now. This holiday was getting totally out of control.

My stomach was in knots, so to take my mind off the coming encounter, I looked around, knowing Hannah would quiz me on the details.

Frau R.'s bedroom had been in the west wing, overlooking the river. I was in the east wing, on the back side of the house. Out the window I could see rolling foothills covered with snow. The room was large, with a high ceiling and ornate plaster molding water-stained from years of leaking roofs. I thought it was best to stay put and didn't even peek down the corridor for fear Frau Director might be watching.

Satisfied that I had done my job as observer, I took a seat

behind the big desk in the middle of the room. Naturally curious, I tugged on the drawers and found them locked. Rows of metal filing cabinets stood against the wall, and I got up to check them out. Maybe I could sneak a peek at Poppy's file.

Keeping one eye on the door, I tried each file cabinet drawer, determined now to get a look and learn what I could about his family. All locked. A set of keys hung by the door, but before I could try any of them I heard a little knock. Poppy opened the door and nervously waited for permission to enter.

My heart stopped at the sight of him. He had a crooked little smile instead of tears, but his head had been shaved, too, since I saw him Thursday, and he looked even more fragile. The clothes hanging on his body had obviously not been purchased with him in mind; his shirt was too long and his pants too short. They were colorless and dirty. I greeted him with a lump in my throat I couldn't get up or down. *How can this bright, eager little boy be imprisoned here?* I thought as I shook his bony hand. A fantasy of escape crossed my mind. I wanted to take him right then and walk straight out of the horrible place. The ambassador would surely help us protect him. Or Mom would gladly take him in. I was planning our escape from Iasi before we even sat down to talk.

He rubbed the stubble on his head. "Bugs," he explained, ashamed.

"Um . . . yeah . . . ahhh . . ." I mumbled, totally at a loss for a quick reply. Despite my fantasy, I knew I couldn't get out the front door, let alone back to Iasi and out of Romania with Poppy. So I motioned him to join me on the floor and we sat down together, cross-legged, on a worn-out rug. I handed him the plastic bag I'd brought.

"Wow," he said, holding the sweat shirt. "Wow!" again, only much more excited, when he saw the cap. He slapped it on at once and grinned at me. Poppy was instantly more comfortable in the baseball cap. It hid the shame of his shaved head and gave him a little dignity.

"Now I . . . am . . . you," he said. I took that to mean "I look like you."

Except for the scars on your cheek and chin and the sunken, pale skin stretched over your protruding bones, I thought, smiling through my nervousness. "Just like me," I agreed and helped him pull on the sweat shirt.

It came down to his knees, and his hands disappeared in the sleeves. We both laughed, but he sat back down and snuggled in the warmth of the heavy sweat shirt, thanking me with his eyes.

"Tell me about you," I said, speaking slowly and using some hand gestures.

"My name is Poppy," he said. "Ma numesc Poppy." He patted his chest, teaching me the phrase in Romanian.

"Ma numesc Constantine Kaye," I responded, giving him my full name. "Just call me Con."

"I am Gabriel Popa. But call me Poppy," he said, catching on quickly.

I had never heard his first name before, only his nickname. "Gabriel?" I asked, amazed at the coincidence.

"Yes, Gabriel." He nodded, losing interest in this line of conversation as he looked at the book I had brought him.

I knew Matthew had taught Poppy to read a little English, and I thought he would enjoy the pictures even if he couldn't understand all the words of my Asterix comic book. I handed him a copy of my favorite, *Asterix the Legionary*.

"Wow!" he exclaimed, hugging it to his chest.

"Cool," I said, teaching him a new word.

We sat there for a while as I told him the story, reading part of the text, explaining the pictures. He laughed, not at the jokes, but when I laughed. And he ran his finger carefully over each page as if it was a thing of beauty.

"Cool," he tried his new word when we finished.

I pulled out a piece of Jolly Rancher candy, one for him

and one for me, and we shared the sweet moment in silence.

"Cool," he said again, his pleasure so obvious it made me feel guilty about my own never-satisfied appetite. It made me think of the welcome-home chocolate cakes at the Walker Ranch in Wyoming. The deep, rich three-layer chocolate topped with fresh fruit. For some reason I began to tell him about my Gran, who made them for me.

Only as I talked I realized, too late, how terrible it was to tell Poppy—who had no one to love him or make him a special cake, no place to visit, no one to miss him when he was grown—all about my loving family. He couldn't relate to my stories of grandparents, aunts, uncles, cousins. Even a mother or father. Embarrassed, I stumbled over my story and stopped in midmistake. "I'm sorry. I didn't mean to . . ." *Oh, please help me, God. Help me not to hurt him,* I prayed.

Amazingly, this little boy who had nothing smiled at me—who had so much—and understood I hadn't meant to hurt him.

"It's okay. Please tell Poppy about Tată and Mamă and family. I like to know it about you."

So I did tell him. Sitting there in the middle of eastern Europe, I told him about my whole family at the ranch in far-off Wyoming. I pulled a picture of the cousins out of my bill-fold, showing him Lindy, Alisa, Kate, Claire, Jess, and Abby.

"Nice," he said, touching the picture. He pointed to Abby, the youngest of the cousins. "Pretty."

"Yes, she is," I said. "And I will tell her you said so."

I went on to tell him about my brush with the black widow spider, and the bad guys who wanted to take the ranch away from my grandparents.

Snuggled next to me, he ate up every word. I didn't know how much he understood, but when I stopped he wanted more.

"Tell Poppy about your tată." He spoke the Romanian word for *daddy* with such longing it broke my heart and shut my mouth. "Please," he pleaded. "How is it to have a tată?"

Fighting back tears, I swallowed hard, pulled on the bill of my own baseball cap, and began.

"My tată is dead," I said, making sure he understood, thinking how amazingly God had already answered my prayer. I knew how to reach him with the only thing in the world the two of us shared. "My tată died before I was born. I never saw him," I explained as Poppy's eyes grew wide. He felt it, too. We shared this one thing. He understood.

"Did you live in a casa de copii?" he asked.

I was tempted to lie to him, to make him think I understood a little more of his pain. But I couldn't. "No, I live with my mother."

"I am sorry Con has a dead tată."

I accepted the sympathy of my new friend without telling him that now I had a wonderful new father. Not the hero I had dreamed up in my mind, but a real live man who loved me, who had even rescued me from danger once.

Poppy laid his hand on my knee, touching the warm, thick texture of my jeans. I looked at his own threadbare polyester pants.

"And I am sorry for Poppy," I said in a quiet voice, though I actually wanted to shout about the injustice of his life.

Dr. Lavinia opened the door too soon. She frowned at us sitting there cross-legged on the floor talking. I didn't expect much else from Frau Warden.

Poppy looked at me and whispered, "Thanks." No tears. Just resignation.

"Go," she commanded Poppy, pointing to the door. And as he walked obediently past her, she grabbed the Redskins cap and tossed it on her desk.

His face fell. I gasped.

"You can't . . ." I protested, leaping to my feet. Then remembering my tone of voice, I quickly turned on what little charm I had left and politely asked if he could possibly keep the cap for a while.

"No, he cannot keep these gifts. I told you that before. And you must go now, also. Matthew waits for you downstairs."

She had the look of a principal, all right, with her straight back and cold voice. But maybe something in my face softened her just a little because she gave me an explanation of sorts:

"I know you think I am cruel, but I am doing Gabriel a favor. An older boy would have taken the cap. Young Gabriel is a fighter and would have struggled. But in the end he would have lost and been beaten up in the process. Don't condemn things you don't understand, young man. Now go."

Poppy, who probably knew the truth without understanding her German words to me, took it better than I did. As he stood hesitating by the door, he looked back at me with a longing that had nothing to do with a baseball cap. I wiped my eyes lest Frau Director see the moisture forming there.

Striding across the room, past the stony Dr. Lavinia, I leaned down to hug my new friend and impulsively, stupidly promised I would come again.

———————◆———————

"It's terrible, Hannah. Horrible. It's worse than anything we've ever seen. . . . I hated it."

"Okay, calm down, Con. Tell me what was so terrible. Tell me everything." She snuggled into the big, soft sofa in the residency living room.

Several hours, a long shower, and a change of clothes later, I could still taste and smell the casa de copii as I tried to describe it to Hannah. I was in the wing chair facing the fire and shivering despite my warm sweat shirt and the blazing logs.

The drizzle of rain against the window was turning into

pings of ice. Cold from the inside out, I leaned closer to the fireplace, burning my hands and face without warming up at all.

"Poppy probably doesn't even have the sweat shirt I gave him anymore. And that stupid woman took his cap. His head must be freezing. They've shaved the kids' heads. Lice or some dumb thing. He's cold, Hannah, do you understand? Here we sit in this warm, quiet, safe place, and he is cold and probably hungry. And nobody cares."

I put my head in my hands, elbows on my knees, and stared at the floor.

Hannah waited without speaking while I tried to get control.

"I told him I would be back. I know it was dumb, but I couldn't help it. And going back there is the last thing I ever want to do. And yet I want to go back right now. Makes a lot of sense, doesn't it?"

"It does, Con. It makes perfect sense, and next time I'm going with you. We have four days left in Iasi—plenty of time to get in a couple days of good skiing and still go back to Livada de Meri."

"It's not Livada de Meri anymore, Hannah. No golden apples will ever ripen in the sun. Nothing good is left. But I am going back. It will be easier with you. But are you sure? It's horrible."

"Of course I'm sure. We can't not go back. . . . But what can we *do* for him?"

"I think I'll call my mom. She always knows what to do."

"Or Aunt Ruth," Hannah suggested. "Maybe I should tell her about Poppy."

"No, don't do that," I insisted. "If we tell your aunt and uncle about Poppy, we would have to tell them we went to Barsa without their permission when they thought we were sight-seeing in Iasi. Then we might not get to go back at all."

"Hmm," she muttered as I put another log on the fire.

We sat there quietly for some time, wondering.

"Con, has it occurred to you that this whole thing might be more than a coincidence?"

"What whole thing?"

"Well, we found Frau R.'s home, where Andrei *Popa* killed *Gabriel* Levi. And who is living there now but a little boy named Gabriel Popa? I mean, doesn't that seem odd to you?"

I *had* thought of that, of course. And on the way home I had told Matthew about Frau R.'s letter and asked him about the coincidence of names. I gave Hannah his answer.

"There are three thundred and fifty other children living there, too. And both Popa and Gabriel are very common names in Romania. Like John Smith in America. Besides, in case you hadn't noticed, Gabriel was a Levi name, Popa the last name of his killer. Gabriel Popa together doesn't quite fit."

She was not convinced.

"Just listen and try to follow me. What if Andrei Popa also had a baby . . . say, in 1950, after the war and once he'd gotten on with his life. I'll round the numbers off to keep the math simple for you," she teased. "Let's give this Popa baby a name: Andrei Jr. And Andrei Jr. marries a younger woman later in life—say, at age forty, which would bring us up to 1990—then they have a child in the early nineties. That child would be Poppy's age now."

I was a little lost, but she went on anyway.

"What I'm saying here is that Andrei Popa could theoretically be Poppy's grandfather. Matthew said he was abandoned when he was about four years old. It's possible. And they sound like the kind of family that would abandon a child." Hannah pulled her stockinged feet up under her on the couch, leaned back with her arms crossed, and looked very smug, as if she had just aced a test. "Well, what do you think?"

I thought she was crazy and didn't like her theory.

"I understood there would be no math on this holiday," I said, dodging the question.

She threw a pillow at me, jumped up to get a pencil and piece of paper, then wrote the following:

The Time. The Place. The People.

Andrei Popa, Iron Guard: killed Gabriel Levi 1942 at Livada de Meri (Barsa, Romania).
Son Andrei Jr.: born 1950, died—?
Grandson Andrei III (Poppy?): Born between 1992 and 1994, abandoned around 1996 and placed in orphanage at Livada de Meri.

"Same last name, same town, the same kind of people—people who might abandon a child. I mean, we're not talking about the cream of society here. Mathematically, it is possible."

"No. I mean yes. Your math is fine. Your reasoning is rotten, in more ways than one. First of all, Poppy's first name is Gabriel, not Andrei. Why would the name Gabriel get passed down through that family? Not a very likely choice. And—"

"Wait a minute," Hannah jumped in. "You said Gabriel is a common name. So that *is* a coincidence. Who says Andrei Popa had any say in naming his grandson?"

She handed me the piece of paper. "See, it works."

I had actually—momentarily—thought it possible myself. But I had looked in the eyes of Poppy, and I didn't believe he could be the grandson of an anti-Semitic, murderous thug.

"Is this supposed to make me feel better?" I waved the paper at her. "If your theory, which we couldn't prove anyway, is correct . . . do you realize what that would mean for Poppy? What it would do to him to find out this kind of stuff about his family? You don't understand, Hannah, but I know what it's like. All those years before Mom married Nigel, I used to daydream about how my dad died a hero instead of in an airplane accident. It would be awful, even now, to find out something terrible about him. Last summer when I learned what Grandpa Walker had done for the Shoshone tribe, I felt like I was part of it somehow. I felt proud being part of the same family. Think how I would have felt if I'd learned he had robbed and cheated Native Americans. No, I think your theory stinks. And even if it's true, I don't want Poppy to know. It's better not even having a family."

"Okay, okay. I wasn't suggesting we go tell him. But we did agree to find out what happened for Frau R. And we did find her house, with someone living in it by the same name as the murderer. It *is* a possibility, given the facts. That's all I'm saying. Let's follow the lead we have, that's all. See what we can find out about his family from the orphanage file. . . . See? That's all I'm saying."

I did begin to see.

"Maybe we could ask Matthew to read his file, see what relatives are listed. I actually tried to look at his file today, but the file drawers were locked."

"Con! That wasn't bright. What if you were caught?"

I shrugged. "I'll call Ovi and get Matthew's number. It wouldn't hurt to ask. Maybe we could at least trace the murderer, if not the baby. I would love to know if that creep Andrei Popa is still alive and pay him a visit."

"All right, Con!" Hannah leaped off the couch and gave me a huge hug, which I didn't mind a bit, and went off to the kitchen to get us some Coke.

The Goldbergs hadn't returned from their outing to a local monastery. And Andrew Hart still hadn't shown up with Hannah's photographs. The ambassador wasn't going to be happy.

Glad I had pleased Hannah and finally warming up and relaxing, I picked up a brochure from the coffee table and read about the ski resort where we would finally hit the slopes tomorrow.

"Con," Hannah said, handing me a Coke, "I agree it's a total long shot. But thanks. This is going to be fun. Like our old days of following people around in Vienna. Only this time, think what we could find. And since we got zero on the Levi family from Rabbi Altar, this seems our only lead. And if we can't find out what happened to Gabriel's baby, maybe we can at least find out what happened to the man who killed him."

"And maybe we could get the book back from him for Mia," I added, totally kidding.

"Exactly. Oh, Con, just think what we might learn from Poppy's file. We might be able to find and confront the man who killed Frau R.'s Gabriel."

She was taking this stuff way too seriously.

"Forget it," I said, remembering Poppy's trusting face. "Forget the whole thing. I'm sorry I mentioned it. We are not going to use Poppy as a pawn to satisfy your obsession about some imagined romantic story or find some old book."

"This *is* a romantic story, and it's not about some old book," she shot back angrily. "And you know it. Have you forgotten about justice? If Poppy's grandfather killed Gabriel, he is guilty of murder and should be brought to justice. I seem to recall you wanting to confront him with news of a living eyewitness."

"Oh please, it was in the middle of the night on a train. I was tired. I tend to make rash statements, remember? And besides, that was before I met Poppy. I am not going to stir up anything that would make his life *worse*. No way."

"It *is* a lead we should follow," Hannah said stubbornly. "That's all I'm saying. And I don't know why Poppy would ever have to know."

Maybe it was the warm fire, or Hannah's serious face, but in the end I gave in, with the firm belief that Matthew would never get any farther into those locked drawers than I had.

"Okay," I said. "I agree as long as everyone knows Poppy is not to be affected."

"That's what I'm saying," she assured me, handing me the phone.

I took my time explaining all the bits and pieces to Matthew, things I had left out today in the car. I even read him the whole letter over the phone. Matthew listened, politely at least, and then much to my surprise agreed to see what he could do.

"It is actually against the law to look at those records without permission, but upon occasion Dr. Lavinia shows me a child's file for various reasons. I might manage it . . . if you agree not to use the information in any way that might jeopardize my position working in the orphanages." Before hanging up, Matthew said, "By the way, did you notice a black Peugeot following us at any time today? On the way to the orphanage or in Barsa on the way back?"

"No," I said, a prickly sensation running along my spine. "What do you mean 'following us'?"

"Oh, it's probably nothing, but you see so few foreign cars in Iasi. You know, mostly Dacias."

I felt my breath getting shallow as he went on.

"Well, I think I remember the black Peugeot passing us on the way there. And I know one followed me for some time on the way back and passed me again about the time we hit Iasi. I wouldn't have thought anything of it, but a black Peugeot has driven slowly past my apartment at least twice this afternoon since my return. You seem to notice cars, and I just wondered."

I had been so nervous on the way to the orphanage, and totally preoccupied on the way back, that I wouldn't have noticed a Lamborghini Diablo if it had crawled up our tail pipe.

"Probably nothing, then," he said when I didn't answer.

"Just my imagination. I'll try to get your info on Poppy on Monday. Happy skiing!"

Probably nothing, I agreed. But that didn't stop the knot of fear in my stomach from growing to the size of a football. Staying at the ambassador's residency in Iasi wasn't exactly hiding out, and Dirty Harry was trained to stake out places that have guards as good as the U.S. Marines. I was eager to have Andrew Hart show up with Hannah's photographs of the demonstration so I could look for Grunwald's face in the crowd.

"What did he say?" Hannah asked when I got off the phone. "Will he do it? Will he look at Poppy's file? Con. . . ? You look a little pale. Something wrong?"

"No . . . nothing's wrong. And yes, he'll try."

"Hurray! We're on our way, Con. This is so cool."

Pleading tiredness, I went upstairs to my room. I needed to be alone, to think. Trying to wipe out the idea of Dirty Harry staking out the residency and chasing me in a black Peugeot, I forced myself to focus on another idea—one so bizarre I didn't dare tell even Hannah.

Late that night I crept silently down to the phone in the kitchen. I had a snack to help me think and then called my mom. She listened silently, and to my surprise I heard tears in her voice when she replied, " 'Love your neighbor as much as you love yourself.' Whoever this little boy is, he is your neighbor, Con. Thanks for loving him. I'm very proud of you."

And then—as I knew she would—Mom gave me an idea of how to help him.

A FACE IN THE CROWD

YOU COULD CUT THE TENSION WITH A KNIFE MONDAY morning at the residency. Andrew Hart still had not shown up with Hannah's developed film. After our great day of skiing Sunday, with nothing to worry about except making it to the bottom of the slope without hitting a tree, reality had returned with the morning light. Many shops had closed early on Friday because of the demonstration, and with nothing open over the weekend, Andrew had failed to get the film developed. He had promised to be at the shop this morning, waiting for the door to open.

The idea of one-hour developing clearly had not reached Iasi, because there was still no sign of him at eleven o'clock. Uncle Aaron had a room full of impatient VIPs waiting to examine the pictures. These men—an Interpol agent from Hungary and two very tired-looking State Department types—were not at all pleased to have traveled great distances only to find there was no evidence to be viewed.

Hannah and I were finishing our hot chocolate in the formal sitting room, watching the tension rise.

"My man will be arriving at any moment," Ambassador Goldberg calmly assured everyone. "He is on the way here now with the developed film."

And heaven help Andrew Hart if he misses this "train," I

thought. I raised my eyebrows and started to say, "Don't count on him," but Hannah told me to be nice and give the poor guy a chance.

I looked around, enjoying the drama. Filling up the wing chair by the window was the Interpol agent from Budapest, Lazlo Szegedi. He was built like a linebacker whose muscle had long ago turned to fat, including his cheeks, which had drooped to jowls. But the mind was still tough, according to Uncle Aaron, who said Lazlo Szegedi was a match for any terrorist and feared by all of them.

Szegedi had put away many an Odessa member, and I knew one of the men on his most-wanted list at the moment would be the recently escaped terrorist Hans Grunwald. His hard mouth, set in a frown, didn't invite conversation, however, and I kept quiet.

Mr. Interpol Agent had been on a ski holiday in the Austrian Alps when his office tracked him down and told him to hotfoot it to Romania. He didn't look pleased to be off the slopes.

But his temper would improve, I figured, if the developed film brought him closer to his prey.

On the sofa sat Mr. Wohlers and Mr. Smith, U.S. terrorism experts Uncle Aaron had summoned from Bucharest. Ovi had picked them up at the train station and delivered them directly to the house without a stop at the hotel for them to shower and shave. They looked about as fresh as last week's fish, with rumpled suits and day-old beards. Complaining to their boss was probably not a good career move, so they waited silently, if not patiently.

"Don't know why they look so glum. At least the pigeons missed *them*," Hannah whispered to me.

Wohlers and Smith were in charge of keeping track of radical elements currently thriving on the fringes of Romanian society, Uncle Aaron had explained to us at breakfast. Anti-Semitic groups were popping up all over the former Communist countries, using the same old propaganda of blaming the Jews for everything. Despite the fact there were almost no Jews left in Romania or any of the other former Eastern bloc countries, the strategy was working, and Uncle Aaron and the State Department wanted proof of outside agitators in order to pressure the Romanian government to take action against this danger.

Everyone in the room had good reason to be interested in Hannah's pictures. And Uncle Aaron was counting on them. Based on our description of the event, he expected her film to justify his summons of Szegedi, Wohlers, and Smith. The ambassador needed to show clear documentation of old Iron Guard members returning to Romania to honor a former comrade, young neo-Nazi punks happy for any occasion to demonstrate their anti-Semitic and antidemocratic views, and professional terrorist agitators there to destabilize the government.

The ambassador wasn't going to look too good if the photos were a flop.

Minutes passed, tensions rose. Still no Mr. Hart, no pictures.

Finally the Hungarian detective exploded.

"I can't believe you haven't even seen this 'evidence' yet!" Lazlo shouted. "What if the stupid pictures didn't even turn out? Did you think about that, Mr. Ambassador, before you dragged me all the way over the blooming Carpathian Mountains?"

Uncle Aaron, not easily ruffled, answered calmly. "I have not yet viewed the evidence, sir," he replied with diplomatic tact mixed with authority. "Because I am, as you can imagine, hindered by certain limitations of our location. Iasi is a very beautiful city"—he smiled at Ovi, not wanting to insult Romania—"but getting film developed here over the weekend has proved quite impossible. Do be patient a little longer."

"How long?" the man growled.

"Not long, I assure you. And furthermore, Mr. Szegedi, if I had waited to bring you here until after I reviewed the film this morning, it would have delayed your arrival by at least another day. That is time you can't afford to lose in alerting border guards to the movement of possible suspects out of Romania."

Touché, Mr. Ambassador, I thought, enjoying this little drama. I, too, had good reason to see Hannah's pictures. To see if the face I was looking for—and maybe missed in the crowd—was captured by her film.

"Time to go," Ovi said, pointing to his watch. He had agreed to drive us to the orphanage today so we could meet with Matthew and learn if he had seen Poppy's file. Uncle Aaron, who wanted us out of the way for his big meeting, had cheerfully agreed to our outing with Ovi without questioning our exact destination.

The ambassador nodded for us to go.

"Can't we wait a few minutes and see the pictures before we go?" I asked, not wanting to miss out on the excitement here.

"Request denied," he replied. "All nonessential personnel out!"

Hannah tried again. "Couldn't we stay for a little while and sort of help out? I mean, we were there and might be able to explain things."

"Sorry, Hannah, your descriptions will be helpful later. But our discussions will be sensitive, and all information from the film will be on a purely need-to-know basis. You really don't need to know, so take off and have fun."

I definitely did have a need to know and toyed briefly with telling the ambassador why. But if I explained that I had seen Hans Grunwald's ugly face on the train and wanted to see if he was in the pictures, that would be the end of our trip to Livada de Meri. In order to keep my promise to Poppy, I had to keep my mouth shut. Besides, Hannah was counting on us tracking down the Popa family from Poppy's file. She would kill me if I messed up that opportunity.

"Try not to do anything stupid while you're in Romania," Mom had said to me as she waved good-bye at the train station in Vienna and again last night on the phone.

I rubbed my hands together nervously, cracked my knuckles, and wondered if I wasn't about to do something very stupid indeed by not telling Uncle Aaron my concern about Grunwald, including the black Peugeot that had followed Matthew and me from Barsa on Saturday.

Oh well, I decided, *it won't be the first time in my life I have done something stupid, and it probably won't be the last.* I would look for Grunwald in the pictures tonight, leaving plenty of time to tell the Hungarian terrorist-hunter one of his prey was in town.

"Just have a snack before you go," Aunt Ruth said, coming in with a tray of coffee and sweet breakfast bread to calm the nerves.

Ah, the power of food, I thought, taking two pieces. *Calms the soul, occupies the mind.* At least my mind most of the time.

"Hannah, you did remember to take off the lens cap during the demonstration, didn't you?" I asked in a voice loud enough to be heard by all the nervous guests. A little hand grenade to liven up the group.

It exploded right on target.

"*This* is the photographer you sent to the demonstration?" Mr. Hotshot Investigator exploded at the ambassador. "A mere child? You brought me *here*, off the ski slopes of Austria, because of some pictures taken by *her*?" He was livid, jowls swinging as he shook his head like a charging bull.

"Hey, calm down." I jumped to my feet to undo the damage. "I was only kidding. When you see the pictures, you will be thanking your lucky stars this 'mere child' was around to take them. And put her life on the line doing so, I might add."

"And he"—Hannah stood up by my side and came to my defense—"risked his life protecting me while I took the photographs. See?" She pointed to the thin red cut not yet healed on my neck. "You'll be thanking us later, even if we are only 'mere children,' Mr. Szegedi!"

Wohlers, Smith, and the ambassador seemed ready to join in defending us against the inspector when the sound of a car screeching to a halt in the gravel broke into the explosive atmosphere. Through the window I could see Andrew Hart fly out of the car and up to the door, his tie and trench coat flapping as he ran.

"Ahh," Uncle Aaron said with a twinge of relief. "Let's retire to my office. I believe we can begin. And, Ovi, return the kids safely by dinner, or I'm in trouble with my wife."

Ovi saluted and we gathered our things to go.

The bullish Szegedi strode angrily after the ambassador, muttering Hungarian oaths, followed by a very nervous Andrew Hart and the resigned Wohlers and Smith to examine the evidence in the privacy of Uncle Aaron's office upstairs.

"Hungarians," Ovi explained, helping Hannah on with her jacket, "are sometimes not gentlemen."

"Never mind, Ovi, it's okay. Con shouldn't have riled him." She smacked me on the back. "When will you learn to let sleeping dogs lie?"

"Sleeping dogs? Please to explain this," Ovi asked as we pulled out of the residency in his old Dacia. The Mercedes, Uncle Aaron explained, was for official use only, not sightseeing trips by relatives.

While Hannah explained the sleeping-dogs Americanism to Ovi, I looked around for lurking black Peugeots as we pulled onto Primaverii Boulevard.

Seeing nothing but other little Romanian cars, I settled in for an uneventful ride, ready this time and even eager to see Poppy and find out what Matthew had learned from his file.

Matthew, whom we had not expected to see until later, stood leaning against his car, blocking the drive leading up to the casa de copii.

His face flushed with excitement, Matthew rushed over to us before Ovi even came to a full stop.

"Listen," he said. "Don't bother to get out. Plans have changed. Follow me to the café where we first met. I have something exciting to tell you."

Without giving us a chance to agree, he was off. Ovi turned the little Dacia around in the drive and followed.

"In chess game, Matthew is good queen, right?" Ovi remarked, enjoying the excitement.

"No kidding," Hannah agreed, practically leaping out of her skin. "It must be good. He must have found out Poppy's past, or he wouldn't be so excited. Oh, I can feel it, Con. We are getting close."

"Yeah—close to the river. Watch out!" I shouted at Ovi, who took the tight turn too wide and slid in the mud dangerously close to the edge. Straight down was the ice-covered Prut. We could hear a groaning sound as ice moved against ice, breaking up along the bank. Soldiers manning the border post were hunkered down inside their drab blue coats and lamb's-wool hats, unsmiling and miserable in the winter wind.

"Don't worry, be happy. Ovi is in control." He laughed, sticking closer to the center of the road. Probably funny in his own language, he was hilarious in broken English.

"You know," he said in his rapid-fire speech, "God make Romania very beautiful. Very nice mountains, rivers. Beautiful country. Birds, animals, everything nice. So then God thought maybe is not fair, Romania got all nice things, other countries in world won't be so happy. You understand?"

"Maybe," Hannah replied, obviously wondering where he was going with this one.

"Okay, then," Ovi said, already chuckling at his own joke. "God make Romanian people, and everything, it is even."

Not sure I should laugh at the joke at his own expense, I kinda winced and held on as he swerved around a farmer pulling a cartload of hay with a thin brown horse.

"Sorry, Ovi," Hannah said. "I don't get it. I mean, I'm sure it's funny, but I don't get it."

"Uh, Hannah, I think he's suggesting that the people of Romania have messed up big-time, so what God made good isn't looking so great now."

"Right," Ovi nodded. "Con gets my jokes."

He did have a point. The whole country was rusting, crumbling, and rotting away.

"Well, it's not your fault—not the Romanian people's fault," kindhearted Hannah insisted. "After fifty years of Communism, what do you expect? It will take a long time to undo the damage done by Ceausescu. Uncle Aaron said so."

Ovi's car coughed to a stop outside the café, where Matthew was already waiting.

"Hurry up," he said. "I've got news I'm dying to tell you."

It was getting colder. A few flakes of snow had begun to stick to the road and dust the car with white. I was glad we had brought another warm sweat shirt for Poppy. He would need it for our walk, and I was happy enough to pass along another one of mine.

We stepped inside, and Hannah picked a table by the window. She moved an ashtray full of cigarette butts and old ash to another table and wiped crumbs off the plastic tablecloth as Ovi called an order to the waitress.

"Okay already, you can stop cleaning now and listen up," I told Hannah.

Matthew finally calmed down enough to begin his story. "I arrived early this morning to find Dr. Lavinia in her office. She readily agreed when I asked to see some files. And you wouldn't believe what I found out. . . ." He paused momentarily when the waitress came with our Cokes, rolls, and cheese.

"Time for serious business now," Ovi said, patting his stomach and digging in.

"Go on, man. What did you find out?" I said, ignoring the food.

"Well, it's pretty amazing, actually. Gabriel Popa was born on August 31, 1993, and was left at the orphanage in 1996. The papers were not signed by a parent, but by his grandmother. Her name is Monica Popa and . . . Are you ready for this?" He paused dramatically.

"Matthew, if you don't get on with it . . ." I threatened as Hannah and I both leaned across the table aggressively.

"Okay, okay," he said, a little taken aback. "Monica Popa is still alive, *and* she is living near here at the state old folks home. You can go visit her today if you want."

"Yahoo!" we shouted.

Hannah pounded on my arm in excitement. "Do you realize what this means, Con?"

Matthew was a little shocked at the eruption he had just caused and tried to calm us down. "Hey, don't get your hopes up. That doesn't mean Monica Popa is the widow of Andrei Popa. It just means Poppy's grandmother is here and you can talk to her. It's exciting, but that's all. And, Con, no, he is not eligible for adoption."

Mom had suggested last night that I find out if Poppy was legally abandoned, which would make him eligible for adoption.

Hannah charged ahead on the Andrei Popa theory, pumping Matthew for any other information from the file.

All I could think about was the unfairness of the situation. *Poor little Poppy,* I thought over and over. "Wait a minute. What about Poppy? Wasn't he expecting us?" I asked, remembering the original plan.

"Not yet," Matthew explained. "When I read the file this morning, I knew you would want to go see the grandmother first. So I made arrangements for you to take Poppy out for a walk in the woods this afternoon."

Matthew then went on to explain everything the file had told him: "Poppy's grandmother has never been to visit him. He has no record of any visitors. But she does inquire about him once every six months by letter. According to the law, any contact by a family member occurring at least every six months satisfies the requirement to remain the legal guardian of the child. That means the child is officially unadoptable. It is a legal limbo for thousands of kids like Poppy. Even though she never visits him, and she must be very old and probably cannot visit, she manages to write often enough to prevent his adoption."

"But what about his mom and dad? Are they alive? Do they visit?"

"I'm sorry, Con, but Monica Popa is listed as Poppy's only living relative. There was a small notation that the parents died in 1993—the year Poppy was born. His grandmother must have tried to raise him until 1996, and then was probably too old to care for him and took him to the orphanage. He has not had a visitor since he was brought to the orphanage at three and a half years old."

I couldn't imagine it.

"Last year I actually inquired about his legal status, wanting to find a family to adopt him. He is so bright and would thrive in a home. Dr. Lavinia told me then he wasn't on the 'adoptable' list. I didn't have a family interested at that point, so I didn't pursue any details about his situation. But it is now clear that as long as Mrs. Popa is alive, Poppy is stuck in the system unless she agrees to sign the abandonment papers. The record shows she wrote to him only two months ago. She is being very careful to keep her legal authority over him, it seems."

"That's a horrible law," Hannah said furiously. "Someone can sign a child over to the state, never come to visit or take care of him in any way, but still keep him locked up in there!"

She was fighting back tears.

Ovi looked uncomfortable at the unfairness of such a system in his own country.

I was shocked, too. My plan had just gone down the tubes. When I called Mom last night and told her about Poppy, she had promised to help find a home for him if adoption was an option.

"People are trying to change the law, but for now there is no way around it," Matthew said. "But hey, you wanted to talk to this woman about your mystery, right? Well, go see her, find out her husband's name and if he was an Iron Guard commander. You can still go see Poppy this afternoon. He will be thrilled to have you visit him. And I will continue to watch out for him, do the best I can."

"No offence, Matthew, but that isn't good enough," I said. "Maybe we can convince her to sign the legal papers. Otherwise he's stuck in that horrible place for who knows how long. Unless she's dead by now. She must be in her nineties. Probably can't even remember if she had a husband, let alone what he did half a century ago."

"Possible," Matthew said. "But she sounds to me like she is still aware enough to contact the orphanage on a regular basis. That does not suggest total senility."

"But it also doesn't suggest a sweet old lady in a rocking chair who will sign on the dotted line to release Poppy if we asked—or tell us if her husband murdered Gabriel Levi," I countered. "But it's the best lead we are likely to get. Let's go to this old folks home and see this Monica Popa."

"I have a class at the orphanage, but why don't you visit Monica on your own. Just ask your questions about her husband rather carefully," Matthew advised. "She may be very sensitive if he was an Iron Guard legionary."

"Oh, we'll be careful," Hannah said, getting excited again about the prospect of talking to the widow of Andrei the murderer. "If she gets tense, Ovi can tell her a joke! Okay, Ovi?"

"Sure," he said, downing the last hard roll smeared with butter. "She will tell Ovi all."

Eager to get going, I stood up, hurrying everyone else. Hannah was determined to find out about the past. I was interested in the future—Poppy's future. And I had no intention of letting Poppy know the truth if we did discover his grandfather was Andrei Popa. I wanted to know about Andrei Popa, too. But my main goal in going to see this little old grandmother was to get her to let Poppy go. If we got her to agree, Matthew could go back with the legal paper. And Poppy would be free.

Simple.

Snow was getting heavier by the time we arrived. The state old folks home didn't look like a home of any kind. More like an old school, it was in a large brick structure probably built about the same time as Livada de Meri. And it had the same feel of despair about it. Not eager to see another state institution, I took a deep breath and figured it couldn't be worse than the orphanage.

I figured wrong.

12

THE TRUTH CONCEALED

"IT SHOULD BE A CRIME TO LEAVE YOUR PARENTS IN A place like this," Hannah said as we walked through rows and rows of beds with human flesh under piles of thin, smelly blankets. She had her gloved hand over her nose to try to keep out the smell, breathing through the leather. I had tried that, too. It didn't work. The stench got through and no doubt would remain in our noses for hours.

No one reached out from under their covers. There was an eerie near silence in the room, broken only by the occasional coughing and sniffing. Living dead.

Ovi's shoulders drooped, his eyes down on the floor as we walked. He seemed unable to look at us or the miserable people around us.

Hannah tugged on his sleeve. "Stop that. It's not your fault, ya know."

It wasn't easy, but we kept moving, wishing we hadn't come.

"It's so creepy, Con. Let's talk to her and get out quick, okay?"

Monica Popa, according to the woman at the front desk, was in Women's Ward Five, row twenty-five, last bed.

Few staff appeared as we walked through endless rooms, past row after row of beds. Hannah was gulping back tears and trying not to vomit. We wanted to run.

Finally we came to Ward Five. There was a wooden sign with the number 5 tacked on the door of one more room like the others.

Stepping across the threshold, we looked down the long rows and hurried toward the last row, eager to get this over with and get out. Our feet scraped over the gritty cement floor, past more still bodies huddled under their covers.

"This is it." Hannah gently touched an old woman nearly hidden by a thin blanket in the last bed in the row. *"Pace . . ."* she said, using a friendly Romanian greeting Ovi had taught us.

A shriveled face appeared from under the cover, peering back at us through gummy eyes. A mass of dirty gray hair was matted to her head.

The smell of urine burned my eyes and made my stomach heave.

A gasp escaped from Hannah's throat as she stumbled back from the pitiful sight.

Ovi took over, kneeling down beside the bed. He patted the old woman's hand reassuringly and began, translating for us into English as he went along: "Mrs. Popa, we want to talk to you." He held out the small gift of wrapped cookies and dried fruit he had suggested we bring to her.

There was no response to the question, but her hand darted out, grasping the package and pulling it under the covers.

"We want to talk to you about your grandson," he went on gently.

At that she struggled to raise her head and sit up a little.

"Gabriel? You know my little Gabriel?" Her voice was little more than a raspy squeak. "How do you know my grandson?" Tears began to form in the cracks under her eyes.

"Tell her we met him at the orphanage and want to know if she would let him be adopted," I told Ovi.

One or two other faces began to appear out from under their bedcovers. A shriveled, not very clean hand reached out from the next bed, clutching at Hannah's.

"Oh gross . . . oh no . . ." she murmured, looking at me for help. "I can't."

I stepped back, quickly giving her room to escape.

But instead of moving away, Hannah clasped the cold, dried-out hand and took it into her own warm one, smiling at the lonely old lady who just wanted the warmth of human touch. I stared at Hannah. She had never looked so beautiful to me as she did at that moment.

I forced my attention back to Ovi and his gentle questioning, which so far had produced only more tears from Monica Popa as he explained why she would be helping her grandson if she signed the release papers.

"My son is dead. . . . My son is dead," she moaned. "The accident . . . his wife . . . took them away . . . never returned. All dead. Gabriel is mine. Mine . . . he's all I have left."

"What is she saying?" I interrupted. "What does she mean, the 'accident'?"

"Could be she is confused," Ovi said. "Or maybe her son and his wife die in an accident."

"Go on," Hannah urged him. "Ask about her husband."

First he tried one more time.

"We know you love your grandson. That's why you should give him a chance to get out of the orphanage. Would you do that for him?"

"No," she said, her voice rising. "I won't sign the papers. No one can come back and take him from me. I never had a baby, and you can't take him away. We waited for his mother to come back after the war. She would have taken him. We waited and she didn't come. Now he's mine. Gabriel is mine. . . . I never told anyone about his mother. He is mine, I tell you. No one knows, and I won't let him go. . . . Waited and waited, so afraid his mother would come, but she didn't come. . . . No more after the war. . . ." Her rambling was becoming louder, and as Ovi kept up the translation, I could tell she wasn't making any sense. More people were struggling up in their beds, uncovering their heads and trying to see what was going on.

Oh boy, I thought, *we're losing her.*

"Ask if her husband was in the Iron Guard," Hannah insisted. "We came this far. We might as well ask."

"No, don't ask that yet," I argued. "It'll make her mad, and she'll never agree to sign Poppy's papers." Our whispering only seemed to upset her more. Our chance of learning anything was slipping away from us.

"Maybe it's okay to ask Hannah's question," Ovi said to me. "For some Romanian, Iron Guard is good."

"Okay," I gave in. "Ask her."

But that question produced even more wailing, louder and longer. Shaking her bony finger at us, she practically snarled. "No, no, no. My Andrei was good. He didn't kill no one. . . . You ask a poor old lady wicked questions," she hissed.

Andrei! The name exploded in my brain.

"Andrei?" Hannah and I said together.

She was so angry now that Ovi couldn't understand her latest outburst. He looked around nervously, expecting someone to toss us out for bothering the old woman.

"I think we better go," he said. "Even if her husband is this Andrei you look for, he died years ago. Nobody can't know nothing now. . . ."

Determined not to have come so far and fail, we begged him to try a little more. But it just made things worse. And Monica Popa's outburst was attracting more attention. It was only a matter of time before someone would come to check on the commotion.

Pushing Ovi aside, I knelt down by her bed, looked in her troubled face, and tried the little Romanian I had picked up, begging her to give him a chance.

"I am a friend of Gabriel. Please help him," I begged. "If you love him, let him have a chance to go home."

Something in my broken Romanian calmed the old woman down. She became very quiet again, rubbing her fingers nervously across the blanket pulled up to her neck. She seemed to be considering what I'd said.

Maybe, I thought, I had touched a maternal instinct still alive somewhere in the depths of her soul.

"Da," she croaked, nodding her head. "Da. Da."

I could hardly believe my ears. Hannah patted my back excitedly. "You did it, Con!"

Ovi started to explain that an official from the orphanage would bring the paper for her to sign, while Hannah and I thanked her.

"*Multumesc,* multumesc," we said. But in our excitement, we missed her continued mumbling while she rummaged through a bag of possessions pulled out from under her covers.

"Shh," Ovi said. "She is trying to say something more."

"Oh no, Con," Hannah moaned. "She didn't agree to sign the adoption papers. She thinks you want her to give her grandson something, and that's what she is looking for in that filthy bag. There's nothing in there he could want. Let's go."

"Give Gabriel this," the old woman pleaded. "Not mine, never mine. Give it to Gabriel. . . . It was a present for Gabriel. . . ."

Horrified, we stared at the small package wrapped in old brown paper and tied with string. Monica Popa was holding it out to us, begging us to take it.

"He doesn't want that," I said, disgusted. "The only thing he needs from you, you won't give him."

We began to walk away.

"Wait," Ovi said. "Take it. Throw it away outside. But don't hurt her more. She is . . ."

We could see what she was: a sick, confused old woman who maybe didn't understand what we wanted her to do.

It was Hannah who in the end reached for it, with her gloves back on, and shoved it into my hands. Neither one of us thanked the miserable woman as she disappeared again under her pile of ragged coverings.

Back through stinking rooms we went, quickly now, eager to be gone. I stuck the smelly package in my coat, zipped it up, and wished we had never come. How could I look at Poppy now and know we couldn't give him any more than a picnic in the woods and warm clothes he couldn't keep?

"We failed," I said.

"Miserably," Hannah agreed.

We had met the widow of Andrei Popa—maybe even the Andrei Popa who had killed Gabriel Levi. But she had led us no closer to what Frau R. wanted so much to know—what had happened to the baby boy born at a very bad time in history. Like millions of others, he had disappeared into the flames of the Holocaust, fate unknown.

The snow was really coming down when we emerged into the pale light of day. Standing on the cement steps taking big, deep breaths of air—trying to get rid of the taste and smell of that place—I looked, halfheartedly, up and down the street for the mysterious black Peugeot. Nothing but plain little Dacias sliding around on the increasingly slippery roads.

In quiet depression I crawled into the backseat of Ovi's car and headed for my last visit with Poppy.

"That thing stinks, Con. Toss it," Hannah said from the front, equally depressed about our failure to help Poppy or Frau R.

I pulled the small package out of my pocket. Something made me unwrap it before it joined the other litter on the Romanian countryside.

And when I did, I lost my breath. "Han . . . Han . . . Hannah . . . look." I could hardly get the words out.

There in my hands was a moldy, leatherbound book of Psalms, with shining, bright gold leaf covering the fore edge. There in my hands was Frau R.'s precious book. The book she had given her friend on the day he died.

Hannah and I screamed for joy. And Ovi nearly crashed.

"Stop the car! Pull over, Ovi. Stop." We were shouting and waving our arms and totally confusing our good friend, who nevertheless managed to get off the road.

"Somebody could get not so healthy, you understand," he said sternly. "You scream, I jump, we nearly didn't have so much safety. Mr. Ambassador will not be pleased, I think, if you are hurt."

My hands were shaking as I held the book between my thumb and index finger and slowly spread the edge. The gold disappeared, revealing Livada de Meri in all its former glory, with a little girl sitting under a tall birch tree reading a book. The watercolor painting was as brilliant and beautiful as the day it was snatched out of the dead fingers of Gabriel Levi.

"Cool," Ovi whistled in appreciation of its beauty, using the new word we had added to his English vocabulary. "And—" He stopped, pointing to the house. "That place is now casa de copii, yes?"

Hannah nodded. Ovi looked extremely confused.

"You know what this means, Con. My theory is true. This is absolute, positive proof that Poppy's grandfather killed Gabriel, stole the book, and kept the most valuable thing he and his wife probably ever had right up to the end of her miserable life, in that miserable little bag. I'm sorry for Poppy, but you know it's true. His grandfather was an Iron Guard anti-Semitic fascist. . . ."

She took my silence for pain.

"You don't have to tell him, Con. He doesn't ever need to know what kind of man his grandfather was. But we found it. Just think what it is going to be like to put this back in Frau R.'s hands."

"You must give to Poppy the book," Ovi reminded us, a little confused. "His grandmother said it was a gift for him."

"It's more complicated than that, Ovi," Hannah said. "How could we explain where it came from without explaining how his grandfather got it? Not a good plan. Besides, it belongs to Frau R. Con and I will give it to her," she declared. "That's where it belongs. We can give her back a little bit of her home."

"No, it belongs to Poppy," I said, feeling very happy all of a sudden. "You were wrong, and I was right!"

I felt like singing and dancing all at the same time. But space was a problem in the Dacia, so I simply grinned—a most contented grin.

"Con? Excuse me. What are *you* right about? Or happy about, for that matter? We just learned Poppy's grandfather killed Gabriel, and your smug smile looks like you just took my queen."

"Not yours, Hannah, but it is checkmate. I win. You win. . . . And best of all, Poppy wins!"

Ovi broke in to remind us that while this was all quite interesting, he had promised the ambassador to get us home for dinner, so could we stop talking already and go to the orphanage for our snowing walk in the woods with Poppy already.

Hannah was staring at me with an open mouth and, ignoring Ovi, demanded to know what on earth I was talking about.

I pulled Hannah's folded piece of yellow legal-pad paper out of my pocket and asked her for a pen.

"Look," I said, scratching out and writing over names on the notes she had made.

Andrei Popa, Iron Guard legionary: killed Gabriel Levi 1942 at Livada de Meri

"So far we agree." Hannah nodded.

I crossed out her guesses about Andrei Jr. and wrote *Gabriel Levi (the second): born January 17, 1942.*

I opened the book of Psalms and pointed to the date in Frau R.'s own hand.

"Okay, we knew that already, so get to your major point," Hannah said. "Ovi's getting cold. And I think you are crazy."

I got to the point.

Beside the name of Gabriel Levi and his birthdate, I added *raised by Monica and Andrei Popa; father of Gabriel Popa (Poppy); killed, with wife, in accident in 1993.* Then I wrote Poppy's own entry: *Gabriel Popa: born in 1993; raised by grandmother (Monica Popa) until abandoned to orphanage at Livada de Meri in 1996.*

"No way, Con. . . . I know you care about Poppy, but you can't change his past, fit it into some theory that is a product of your fertile imagination."

Ovi, getting colder and more impatient, had been trying to keep up with our argument and began to smile. His English might have sounded funny, but he understood just fine. "I like your plan better, Con."

"I like it, too, Ovi. Only problem is, it isn't true," Hannah said.

"Yes, it is," I assured them, more confident by the minute. "Monica Popa just admitted it."

Hannah, my very bright friend, began to get it.

"Con . . ." she said slowly, her face taking on the excitement I was feeling. "Is it possible. . . ?"

We had definitely lost Ovi at that point, so I went on to explain.

"Saturday when you wrote this stuff about Poppy being the grandson of Andrei Popa, I thought *it* was a wild idea. But there were so many coincidences that it did seem mildly possible. The right time, place, etc. But unlike you, I have met Poppy. I know you think it's crazy, but I *know* he isn't the grandson of the man Frau R. described in her letter. I know it, Hannah.

"So I began to think there might be another possibility. And the math as you figured it would still work the same. I knew you would laugh at me, so I kept it to myself . . . except for mentioning it to Mom on the phone last night. She said she has found that I have pretty good instincts and that fact is often stranger than fiction, so I should check it out. Well, today I was so focused on getting the old woman to sign Poppy's release papers that I almost missed the very thing I was hoping might be true. Poppy's grandmother isn't really his blood grandmother. She raised him for three years and raised his father from a baby—a tiny baby who just missed being circumcised but was a Jewish baby all the same. There isn't a drop of Popa blood in little Poppy. Remember when she rambled all that stuff about never giving him up because she never had a child, and waiting . . . afraid his mother would return to claim him. . . ?"

Hannah nodded, speechless.

I went on. "We all thought she meant waiting for her daughter-in-law—who, like her husband, Poppy's father, must have been killed in the 'accident'—to come back and claim Poppy. But that doesn't make sense. She wouldn't have feared that, she would have welcomed it. Monica was confused today, but in her confusion she admitted more than she meant to. She was childless, wanting children. Then one day her husband came home, showed Monica the book he had taken off the dead man, and told her about the other Jews he found hiding on the Livada de Meri estate. They read the inscription in the book and discovered the man Andrei killed had a newborn child, and figured the widow and new baby would be part of the group rounded up and headed for deportation. It was a chance for Mrs. Popa to have a child of her own. As head of the local Iron Guard, Andrei Popa arranged the 'transports,' so you can be sure he knew when the Jews at

Livada de Meri would be sent away. He could have arranged things to find the baby first."

"I bet Gabriel Levi's widow wasn't given much choice." Hannah picked up the narrative. " 'Give us your child or he dies with you on the transport or in the camp.' It was Rachel Levi the old woman feared would return one day and claim her son. But the book Mia gave Gabriel did, in the end, save his son's life—just not quite as she intended. And the rightful owner of the book is Gabriel's grandson—little Poppy."

Hannah had tears running down her cheeks. She reached over the seat and gave me a hug. "We found him, Con. You're right. I have to hand it to you. For once in your life you have really done it. Let's go back and confront her with the book and see what more she'll tell us."

"Excuse me," Ovi interrupted our joy. "Could you please to explain quickly what to do? I promise to Mr. Uncle Ambassador to have you back at dinner." He tapped his watch. "We have no time for everything."

We discussed our options. Poppy was expecting us today. We couldn't disappoint him, and it was our last chance to spend time with him. Tomorrow we would be on the train home.

"Hannah, how about you call Aunt Ruth and beg her to let us miss dinner and be a little late," I suggested. "Then we'll have time for another visit to the old folks home and plenty of time to tell Poppy a very long story."

"Cool. Find me a phone, please, Ovi."

"Sorry, bad plan," Ovi argued. "Here is better. I take you in casa de copii, drop you off. Then I go speak with Monica Popa. She will talk now to Ovi, I think. Then I come for you by six o'clock. Okay. It's a good plan?"

It was a great plan, and we quickly agreed. Our first stop was a pay phone.

"What did they say?" I asked as Hannah got back in the car, her black hair frosted with snow.

"I don't know. It was a terrible connection. I could only hear broken-up bits of Aunt Ruth sounding a little hysterical. Something about 'Be careful . . . come back . . . it's danger-ous . . .' You know how she worries about us—probably not wanting us to get stranded out here in the snow."

"Um . . . anything else?" I asked, not absolutely certain Hannah had read the hysteria of her aunt correctly. "Did she say anything about the pictures?"

"Hardly, Con. We couldn't even hear each other. You think she's going to discuss what Uncle Aaron and the others found in my photographs?"

Actually, I thought it was very possible that what Aunt Ruth was so concerned about was just that. Lazlo Szegedi would certainly recognize the face of Hans Grunwald if he saw it in the pictures, and that would be enough for the Gold-bergs to want their "darling niece" safely back at home at once. But it was too late to back out now. And not even Dirty Harry was going to keep me from seeing Poppy.

Ovi drove as quickly as the little car would go on the slick roads, and we arrived at the orphanage twenty minutes later.

"Thanks for everything," Hannah said to Ovi as we got out. "Maybe I should try to call Aunt Ruth again."

"No problem. Don't worry, be happy. I will call again for you after I go in old people home."

"Thanks. You're the best, Ovi." Hannah smiled.

"No problem. Why have dog and do your own barking?"

We could hear his chuckle as he rolled up the window and turned the little car around.

Hannah looked puzzled. "What was that about the dog barking?"

"Not a clue. . . . Another Ovi-ism, I guess. Are you ready?"

"As I'll ever be."

13

PASSPORT TO DANGER

THROUGH THE CRACKS

"WE HAVE COME TO SEE POPPY," I ANNOUNCED TO THE unsmiling woman who opened the door. It was the very same woman who had chased us off that first morning and dragged Poppy back inside. She was clearly not pleased to see us again, but the door stayed open.

I was tempted to gloat but thought better of it and kept my polite smile in place as we stepped into the grand foyer, empty now of children. Hannah and I stood there in awe for a moment thinking about all the history echoing around us. There were tears in Hannah's eyes, for the horror of it now or the beauty that once was, I didn't know.

Hannah's backpack was full of all the goodies we had brought along for Poppy. Things to eat and warm socks and a sweat shirt for a walk in the woods. We even used Frau R.'s money to buy him boots. My backpack had a thermos of hot cocoa and cups for all three of us. I was about to introduce Poppy to the joys of chocolate.

"Come on," I said, tugging gently on Hannah's sleeve to move her up the stairs.

Poppy was already in Dr. Lavinia's office.

He ran and hugged me at my knees.

"You come! You come! You come!" he sang out happily.

I wondered how long he had been sitting there in that

office waiting and wondering. Disappointment he could understand; happiness he didn't have much experience with.

"Poppy, this is Hannah."

Unable to meet her eyes, he hung on to me shyly, keeping his head down.

Dr. Lavinia was brisk and businesslike. "I will show you a back entrance so the other children will not see you go. They are not allowed to walk in the woods, of course."

Of course not, I thought. *That would be fun for them.*

"There is a path through the trees that leads to the river," she went on. "You will see a place there in the trees, a little shelter if you wish to get out of the snow."

Some change had taken place in her attitude, it seemed to me. Not friendly, but less hostile. I wondered what Matthew had told her, how he had managed to get her to agree to this outing.

"Here," she said, unlocking a drawer in her desk. She took out the baseball cap. "It might help keep him warm."

"Cool," Poppy said, gratefully covering up the bumps and nicks on his badly shaved head.

He smiled then at Hannah, his face lighting up as she told him how very good he looked.

In his warm socks, new boots, and another oversized sweat shirt, he looked like a different boy. Overcome with it all, he sat gazing at the boots, wiggling his toes in warmth and comfort his feet had never felt before.

Dr. Lavinia watched without a word.

"Very cool alternative look, don't you think, Con?" Hannah said, in love with the little boy already.

We headed down the center staircase, off to our adventure in the woods.

Hannah paused. "It must have been about here where he died," she said to me, looking across the broad hall to the front door, where the Iron Guard legionaries had stormed in and stopped Gabriel Levi from reaching safety through the back door we were about to use.

"Come, you must hurry," Dr. Lavinia said, "before the other children return from dinner."

I tugged on Hannah's arm. The romantic in her wanted to linger over the memory of that sad day.

But Poppy, unaware of all the history or that it was his own, wanted out the door and into the snow, happy enough for the rare opportunity to play.

Snow was still falling, only lightly, as we headed through the woods toward the river. Back and forth, up and down, Poppy raced around in front of us until he tired and shyly took Hannah's hand. I patted my jacket, feeling the book safely inside my pocket and wondering how I was going to explain all this to him.

" 'The more it snows (Tiddley pom),' " Hannah recited the Winnie-the-Pooh rhyme. After saying it once through by herself, she began again, and Poppy and I joined in on the *tiddley pom*s.

The more it snows
(Tiddley pom),
The more it goes
(Tiddley pom),
The more it goes
(Tiddley pom),
 On snowing.
And nobody knows
(Tiddley pom),
How cold my toes
(Tiddley pom),
How cold my toes
(Tiddley pom),
 Are growing.

Poppy giggled as he sang out each *tiddley pom*.

"Is that the river I hear groaning?" Hannah asked.

We stopped in the snowy woods and listened to a distant creaking sound.

"Could be," I agreed. "Sounds like ice breaking up."

Poppy bounced along beside us, exploring things. Although he had lived on the property for four years, he had never been on an outing in the woods.

With all his new clothes, Poppy looked ten pounds heavier and more than a little warmer. But the wind was coming up, and I felt the chill through my heavy ski jacket.

"Hurry, let's get in out of the cold," I said. "And eat. I'm starving."

But Poppy, for whom food had never been a celebration, was more interested in exploring, and we had to stop and look at each new discovery.

Hannah showed him how to make a snow angel and then a small snowman, and we taught him the first verse of "Frosty the Snowman," to which he added some *tiddley poms*.

The grinding sound of ice breaking up against the bank was getting stronger as we neared the river. A small hill kept it from view, but I could hear the sound of soldiers on the border bridge and knew we must be getting close.

Finally, there on the crest of the hill in a clearing in the trees, we saw the small wooden hut just as Dr. Lavinia had said it would be. I turned then to look back toward the house, thinking I should be able to see Mia's old bedroom window that overlooked the river.

What I saw, however, stopped me in my tracks, filling me with such terror I couldn't move. "Oh no . . ." I whispered to myself. "He's here."

Driving up the road to Livada de Meri was the sleek, very distinctive body of a fine French car. A black Peugeot. It pulled around the side of the house and out of sight. But there was no mistake that it was the same car Matthew had described as following us to Barsa on Saturday. The same kind of car that kept cruising past his house later that same evening..

My legs stopped working and I froze to the spot. Literally.

Hannah and Poppy kept going for a few seconds before they realized I wasn't moving.

One look at my face and Hannah knew something was very wrong.

"What?" she mouthed to me silently. "What's wrong?"

"It's him. Dirty Harry's at the house." I could hardly get out the words.

"Not that again . . ." Her words trailed off. We knew each other pretty well, and Hannah could tell when I wasn't kidding.

"Should we go back?" she asked, looking around at our options.

"No! Poppy is not going back." The boy had understood at least Hannah's suggestion of returning, and he made it clear that no evil he could imagine would be worse than going back to his life in the orphanage a moment sooner than necessary. Poppy had been promised a couple of hours of freedom in the woods with us. Nothing we could say would convince him otherwise.

Hans Grunwald had promised once before to find us and kill us. Now he was here and the advantage was all his.

"Sorry, Hannah," I said. "I've done it again."

"No, it's my fault," she said. "I didn't believe you when you saw him on the train. Point is, what are we going to do? We'll never get Poppy to go back one step toward the house until he's had his promised party. And the other way is the river and border, which we can't possibly get across."

"No good going back anyway," I said, trying to breathe, trying to think. "We can't get past the house down to the road without him seeing us. We have to get to the shelter and wait him out."

Poppy's feet were firmly planted in the direction of the

river. There was a great deal of strength still left in him. Though small for a seven-year-old, he was a fighter, as Dr. Lavinia had said. That accounted for the scars. I liked him a lot, and I wasn't about to let Dirty Harry get his hands on him. *Think, Con, think. There has to be a way.*

"We outsmarted Dirty Harry before, Hannah. We'll do it again. That creep isn't going to hurt you or Poppy," I promised, in German so Poppy wouldn't understand. "Let's make a game out of this . . . so Poppy will do what we say quickly."

She nodded. "And the game is. . . ?"

"Ahhh, the game is called . . . Cover Your Tracks." I quickly pulled out my Swiss army knife to cut branches for each one of us from the nearest evergreen tree. Then I bent down and showed Poppy how to walk backward and brush away his tracks at the same time.

"Let's head for the river. That way." I pointed. "Then double back, covering our tracks to the little hut."

Poppy was trying his best, bending down to brush the snow and getting into the spirit of the game.

"No, not yet," Hannah said. "First we run to the river, then we start the game. Follow us."

He did, running after us as happy as before, totally unaware of our panic, of the danger. We reached the top of the rise and stopped at the edge of a steep hill that led directly to the Prut below, pale and icy, groaning as it flowed beneath the frozen crust. Downstream about five hundred yards was the two-lane bridge that joined Romania and Moldova. One lone truck, weighted down and grinding through a low gear, moved across. We watched as it came to a stop on the Romanian side and the driver got out of his truck for the border guards to inspect his load. The smell of coal-oil smoke drifted out of a smokestack on the guardhouse.

I wondered if we could reach the bridge and the border guards, but the riverbank was steep with tangled overgrowth and a barbed-wire fence. Poppy would never make it.

Without any other options, we headed back toward the hut, playing our game and covering our tracks. Poppy thought it made as much sense as angels in the snow or "Frosty the Snowman," so he went along, still singing the occasional *tiddley pom*.

Snow continued to fall as we neared the shelter. With any luck the tracks we had left would be covered soon anyway.

"Are you sure it's him, Con?" Hannah whispered. "Did you actually see *him*?"

"No. Only the car. But I'm sure. I have been telling myself all week I must be wrong, but I'm not. I saw him on that train. He didn't come to Iasi for us; he couldn't have known we were on the train. No, he came for his neo-Nazi buddies and the demonstration. But he must have seen us—or heard about us—when we were attacked in Revolution Plaza. From there, I don't know. But Matthew told me that black car followed us when he brought me here on Saturday. And probably followed him here again today, hoping we might turn up alone somewhere."

Very alone, it turned out. Deep in uninhabited woods next to a frozen river.

We both strained to see through the woods, looking to see if anyone was coming yet from the house. We continued to speak in German so Poppy couldn't understand.

"I'm sorry I didn't tell your uncle. . . . It's my fault once again."

"No, it's not, Con." Hannah motioned for Poppy to follow us inside the hut. "I should have believed you in the first place. Besides, if we had told Uncle Aaron that Dirty Harry was in Iasi, we wouldn't have been allowed outside the door without a marine guard. We wouldn't have found Livada de Meri or Mrs. Popa, or gotten the book back for Frau R. . . . Or met Poppy," she said, patting him on the head. "I would do it again. Wouldn't you?"

As usual, Hannah had a point.

The little wooden building wasn't much more than a shed with piles of junk, rusting machinery, and boxes. Not much place to hide or any way to keep Poppy quiet if we had to.

Don't let him come, Lord, I prayed silently. *Please, don't let him find us.*

I looked out the small window on the southern side, back toward the house. It had been several minutes since I saw the car pull up, and still no sign of anyone approaching through the woods or walking around outside. Which was good. But I hadn't seen the Peugeot leave, either. Which wasn't good at all.

The idea of Dirty Harry with all those kids swarming around him, expecting him to give them candy like Matthew did, would have been funny if I weren't so scared.

"Do you think Dr. Lavinia will tell him about us and where we've gone?"

"Oh, Con, I don't know. Just keep looking. I'll keep Poppy busy." Hannah set out the Styrofoam cups and filled them with Coke. Tired, Poppy had settled down cross-legged on a pile of straw and was looking at Hannah adoringly with his big brown eyes.

He wolfed down his sandwich of ham and cheese and devoured the bag of barbecue chips, savoring his first taste of Coke, followed by his first taste of cocoa from my Thermos. The hot chocolate left a creamy milk mustache on his upper lip.

"It's been half an hour, Con. Maybe Grunwald isn't coming. Maybe Dr. Lavinia sent him away," Hannah offered, taking a turn at the window so I could eat.

"Is looking out a game, too?" Poppy asked, full and happy now, ready for more games.

"No, Poppy. Not a game. Your English is very good," Hanna told him. "Better than Ovi's, actually—"

"Oh no! Ovi!"

"Exactly," she said, more afraid again. "If unsuspecting

Ovi arrives to pick us up before Grunwald leaves, he'll bring him right to us."

"It's only a little after five," I reassured her. "Ovi won't be back for an hour . . . plenty of time for Grunwald to give up and leave."

But we kept a closer watch, praying the black car would drive away.

"What are you looking for?" Poppy asked again, rubbing off his milky mustache and joining me at the window.

"A car," I replied. "A pretty black car."

"I want to ride in car," he said. "Will you take me some- day in car? I won't be afraid. Okay?"

"Haven't you ever been in a car?"

He shook his head, eyes big at the thought.

I couldn't believe it. Poppy had been too young to re- member when he was brought to this place, and he had never been off the property or in a car since. I turned away, unwill- ing to let him see my tears, and smashed the wall with my fist, wanting to yell, swear, or scream at someone.

"Calm down, Con. You'll scare him," Hannah said.

"He has never even ridden in a car, Hannah. How can they treat these kids like . . . worse than criminals." I rubbed my bleeding knuckles.

Hannah stood up and put her arm around my shoulder. Poppy came and stood next to us.

"Let's tell him now," she suggested.

I noticed that even with the new clothes we had given him, Poppy was shivering. I took off my big jacket and wrapped him in it as he settled down on the straw again to listen to Hannah's story.

She told him about a very brave man who once, long ago, worked for the lady who owned the big house, which was not a casa de copii then. Hannah was a good storyteller, and soon Poppy's eyes were growing wide as she told of the bad soldiers coming to take away the nice lady and the good man who saved her life by giving his own.

It was a story simple enough for Poppy to understand, and I couldn't take my eyes off his face as he followed every word, enchanted by the hero who saved the beautiful lady.

From the first time she read Frau R.'s letter on the train, Hannah had turned the story into a fairy tale. She admired Mia for not giving in to what her culture expected of her—to be a pretty face, a socialite. She admired the intelligence and bravery that brought Mia back alone to rebuild the family estate. And most of all, I knew, Hannah admired Frau Rozstoski for risking her life to hide Gabriel and the other Jews from the Iron Guard. And while she left this part out of the story for Poppy, Hannah knew Mia loved Gabriel and never married because she had never loved another.

Poppy wasn't the only one hanging on Hannah's every word. I couldn't take my eyes off her face as she explained that the story was true and the brave man was Poppy's own dear grandfather. His *bunicu*.

Big tears began to roll down Poppy's cheeks. "My bunicu?"

Hannah went on and explained. "Poppy, remember when Con told you his tată died before he was born? Well, your tată is dead, too, and your mamă. But they loved you very much. They would never have left you at the casa de copii. Your grandmother raised you while she could, but she was too old, too sick to take care of you."

It was all too much for him, and he rested his head against Hannah and cried.

"But, Poppy, listen to me," Hannah tried to comfort him. "A long time after Con's tată died, he got another tată. He's a nice man who made Con his son, even gave him his name. We'll help Poppy find a new tată and mamă, too. . . ."

That is, if Ovi succeeds in getting Monica Popa to agree, I thought, hoping Hannah hadn't promised too much too soon.

"Hannah?" I tried to slow her down. "Is this a good idea?"

"Yes," she said fiercely, all the maternal instincts of thousands of years of women rising to the surface. "Yes, it is a very good idea. Oh, Con, listen, I know Uncle Aaron and Aunt Ruth would love to adopt him. She has told me how much they want to adopt a child while they are in Romania . . . and here he is. How could they not? And Ovi will come through. You'll see. He'll get Mrs. Popa to agree."

"I hope so. . . . But to give him false hope . . ."

"This little Jewish boy is going to ask his father the seder questions next Passover in the American embassy in Bucharest. Mark my words."

Poppy was leaning back against her, soaking in the love if not understanding her words.

Overcome with emotion myself, I could wait no longer to show Poppy the book. I dropped to my knees and pulled it out of my jacket. There in the same place where the artist had painted it so many years ago, Livada de Meri appeared again in all its former glory.

Surprised at the miracle, Poppy took the book in his own hands and watched again the gold leaf disappear and turn into a picture.

"My casa?" he asked, studying it carefully, recognizing the house despite its current condition.

We nodded.

I turned to the last page and read the last line in the last Psalm and then the inscription beneath in Frau R.'s flowery script: *"Let everything that hath breath praise the Lord. Praise ye the Lord." For Gabriel Levi, son of my friend, born January 17 in the year of our Lord 1942. Maria Rozstoski.*

"My tată?" Poppy said, pointing to the name *Gabriel.*

"Yes," I said. "This book was given to him, and someday it will be yours, but not yet. One thief snatched it from the rightful owner, and we can't let that happen again." I reached to put it back inside my coat. But I never even got close.

The door crashed open, and Hans Grunwald stood there, grinning. The hunter had finally found his prey. And trapped prey at that. My worst nightmare had finally come true.

Dirty Harry pointed the barrel of his Kalishnikov rifle directly at me.

"You miserable, rotten kid. Now I keep my promise—to both of you. And what is this?" he said in German, poking Poppy with the gun. "Another Jewish brat?"

"Hi, Dirty Harry," I responded, also in German. I tossed the book to Hannah. "Who's on first now?"

The movement and my taunt worked, and he flexed toward me in fury.

"Run, Hannah," I said in English. "Take Poppy and run to the house. Don't stop."

Moving like lightning, Hannah grabbed the skinny little arm and pulled Poppy past Grunwald and out the door.

I jumped left as Poppy and Hannah went right, and unable to grab us both, Grunwald lurched for me but stumbled. I bolted out behind Hannah and Poppy but headed toward the river, away from the house. I heard Grunwald hesitate and cock the gun. Stupidly, I turned and saw it pointed right at my chest.

"If you catch me, I'll tell you who I am and how I found you in Zürich," I said. "Shoot me now and you'll never know. You've been thinking about it, haven't you? Set up by a kid . . . How could it happen to the great Hans Grunwald? Well, shoot me and you'll never know."

It worked. He dropped the gun barrel and lurched at me, raving mad.

I might not have been as tough as the terrorist, but I was faster. Faster and scared, a good combination.

And I knew the way—away from Hannah and Poppy. Back up the hill I ran, dodging trees and heading for the river and the border guards. I figured he wouldn't shoot me with them looking on. It was my only chance.

The ground was slick, but the deep tread of my hiking boots gripped the wet snow enough to keep me upright. Without looking back, I could hear him crashing through the woods behind me and feel him getting close. I could hear his taunts.

"I will get you this time, Constantine. You will not get away."

I figured he might be right. But on I ran, knowing that once he got the answer to who I was, he would keep his promise to put an end to me. And then go back for Hannah and Poppy. I had to buy some time.

"You hide in Iasi behind marine guards. But who guards you now?" he asked, getting almost close enough to grab my coat.

So he *had* been watching me. I wondered how long but figured this wasn't a good time to ask. I was nearly to the top, out of breath and stumbling to stay out of his reach. With one last spurt I hit the ground and rolled over the crest of the hill, skidded down to the barbed-wire fence, hopped it, and then tumbled down the steep embankment until I hit the ice floe at the edge of the river. I was scratched and bleeding but alive.

Screaming in fury that he had been so close and missed me, Grunwald fired from the top of the hill. I felt the ice spray—shattered by the bullet—and stumbled farther onto the rough, frozen crust. I could see the border guards in the distance on the bridge, not knowing if they would see me— or help me even if they did.

"Tell me about prison, Harry," I shouted up at him in German. "Did you make new friends? Any other guys put there by a couple of kids?" I stumbled backward along the edge of the river, keeping my eyes on him. I tried to keep him talking, hoping he wouldn't fire again once he saw the guards on the bridge.

Whether it was the presence of the guards or because he

simply wanted to feel his hands upon my neck instead of shooting again, Grunwald followed me down the slope. Swearing as he stumbled, he dropped his rifle when he finally hit the bottom. The gun slid onto the ice in front of me. Our eyes locked for a brief moment of tense silence. Then he dove toward the weapon on his stomach, grabbed it, turned, and fired.

The bullet whizzed high over my head, wild and way off the mark, followed by a low groan and cracking sound coming from below. The ice was breaking up beneath me. Afraid of falling through into the freezing current, but certain of a bullet if I gave him a clean shot, I took one step farther out onto the river and felt and heard the sickening sound of ice creaking under my weight.

"What's the matter, Dirty Harry? Still can't catch a rotten little kid like me?" I taunted.

It worked. He lunged at me, yelling at the top of his lungs, then slipped and slid past onto thinner ice. I stepped back toward the bank, grasping a limb protruding out over the river. It bent but held as the current pulled the crust beneath me outward with its swift flow.

Still holding on, struggling toward the safety of the bank, I heard a final crack and turned just in time to see Dirty Harry sink into the freezing water as the crust gave way. The rushing current underneath quickly pulled him in, to his death.

Stunned, I watched the spot where he disappeared until the creaking of the ice reminded me I might at any moment follow him. I made one last effort and pulled myself onto the bank. Collapsing from fear and shock and cold, I laid my head in the bracken, unable to think or move or cry for help. The next thing I knew, I heard voices calling my name.

Uncle Aaron and Lazlo Szegedi were crashing down toward me with Andrew Hart—late as usual—right behind. And there on the crest of the hill stood Hannah, silhouetted in the fading winter sun, guarded by a marine and holding Poppy's hand.

Safe at last, I closed my eyes and buried my face in the leaves and snow and mud, and cried.

THE END

NIGEL'S BMW PULLED INTO GROSSGMAIN RIGHT BEFORE noon, and we headed straight for the Vortel. But even my favorite restaurant and the best Schnitzel in the world couldn't take the edge off my nerves. I hardly noticed the food. We were expected at Frau Rozstoski's at three, and the time until then was dragging like a boring class after lunch.

Hannah and I had wanted to tell Mia all our news in person, so we'd kept most of what happened in Iasi secret from her until now. It was spring break, and we had brought more than pictures of Livada de Meri to show Frau R.

Ever since that day in Iasi when I first held Mia's book and knew for sure Poppy was the grandson of Gabriel Levi, I had been dying to tell her all about it and him. But we had waited until we could visit Grossgmain on spring break and tell her in person. I had given her only the briefest report over the phone: *"Yes, we saw a broken-down Livada de Meri.... No, the skiing wasn't great.... Yes, we will bring some pictures...."*

True enough, but not *the* truth. We had brought that with us.

Poppy walked happily between Hannah and me, occasionally running off in pursuit of a butterfly. His new parents, Ruth and Aaron Goldberg, agreed that he should meet Maria

Rozstoski and had let him come with us to Grossgmain.

Hiking up to Schloss Plainburg to kill time was Nigel's idea, so we set off through the sunny but cool March air, up the gentle slope of the Alpine foothills to the old ruins.

New green grass and spring flowers were sprouting up along the path and over the moss-covered stone walls. After some exploration to see that all was how I remembered it, I climbed up onto the highest remaining rampart of the medieval castle and looked down at Grossgmain. I could see my old house and Frau Rozstoski's behind it. Smiling, I patted a small parcel tucked safely inside the pocket of my leather jacket, just reassuring myself it was still there, that it was real.

"I can't wait any longer," I shouted. "I'm out of here."

Hannah, who was even more antsy to get on with our grand surprise than I was, jumped at the suggestion. She had been waiting for this moment ever since first reading Frau R.'s letter.

"I told you we could do it, and you wanted to go *skiing*," she taunted, heading already for the path. "But if you catch me before I get to Poststrasse, I'll let you share the glory."

This was my backyard, however, not hers, and I headed for a shortcut that was definitely not a path.

A little muddy and scratched here and there, I arrived back in Grossgmain out of breath but first. I stopped to wait outside our old apartment, where a year and a half ago Herr Donner had given me the mezuzah and set off the chain of events that had finally ended on the Prut River two months ago. The Swiss chalet-style house looked very much as it had when Mom and I lived there during the first twelve years of my life. The steep, sloping roof and ornately carved wooden eaves framed the window that had been my room. The shutter was tapping gently against the wall in the breeze. Herr and Frau Donner's apartment on the ground floor was still empty, shuttered and locked up tight. Its owners were still on the run from the Austrian Politzei. I peered between the slats into the blackness.

Deep in memories, I didn't hear Hannah come up behind me.

"You cheated," she said, giving me a friendly slap on the back.

Absorbed in thought, I didn't respond for a while, thinking how unfair it was that, unlike his victims, Herr Donner got away. He was probably living on his stolen money in some other beautiful spot.

"I wonder where he is now."

The man who had lived there had been kind to me, played with me when I was a little boy. He had been my friend. He had also been an officer in the Nazi war machine, cheerfully stealing from his Jewish victims before marching them off to their deaths, then living comfortably off their wealth in this house. I shuddered at the memory of the man whose kindness I had accepted, never seeing his evil.

"Con, don't do that to yourself," Hannah said, reading my mood. "And remember what your mom said in the car this morning: Herr Donner may hide from Austrian law, but justice will find him the day he stands before God to answer for his deeds. It's not your fault he befriended you. You were a little kid—how could you know? Let it go."

"I wasn't that little. . . ."

"Let justice roll down like a river." Nigel had quoted the Old Testament prophet Amos to me last year when I was resisting Mom, thinking she was wrong for turning the mezuzah in to the police to help convict Herr Donner. I thought about the millions of Jewish victims killed by people like Herr Donner and Hans Grunwald—men who were driven by hate so strong that they lost their own humanity in the process. And I realized, too, that it was because of the same hate that the Native Americans near my grandfather's ranch in Wyoming—and elsewhere—were treated for years like they were

less than human. I remembered the picture of the sign that hung in Chief Running Wolf's house: *No Dogs or Indians Allowed*. My grandfather had helped to end that discrimination in his part of the world.

The "river" of justice does not always swallow up evil at once as it did with Hans Grunwald. Herr Donner got away. It is our job, Mom told me once, to love mercy, act justly. God, who is not confined to time and space, will sort out the rest.

Frau R.'s wind chime played its familiar tune in the breeze as we passed by her flower garden, our hiking boots scrunching against the loose gravel. The excitement of what we were about to do began to drive out the dark memories; my pulse was pounding. Hannah must have felt it, too; her face was flushed as she pressed the doorbell.

Then she was there, bent over the metal walker, head held high, a smile on her aristocratic face. I hugged Mia, stooping to reach her frail, shrunken frame, careful not to squeeze too hard. The familiar scent of her starched clothes and old-fashioned face powder were a sweet reminder of my childhood.

Happy greetings completed, Hannah and I moved down the narrow hall into the book-lined sitting room I knew so well. Mia waved to the others and waited for them to come up the walk.

"Look, Hannah. This is the photograph I told you about. It's the count and countess holding baby Mia on her christening day. . . . It's all she has left from Livada de Meri—"

"*Had* left," Hannah interrupted. "It's all she *had* left." She took the silver frame from me and looked closely at the faded photograph of Mia's family.

"The count is kinda cute!"

"Oh please, not again with the kinda cute," I groaned. "Now, the countess . . . *that* is what I call cute. I bet Mia looked like her as a young woman. She must have been very beautiful."

"Never," Frau Rozstoski said, entering the room at that moment and overhearing my remark. "My mother was beautiful. I was interesting at best. But never mind; it got me through." She laughed. "But I want to know, Constantine . . ." Her voice took on that slightly cross tone I knew so well when she used my full name. "I want to know why you did not inform me you were bringing a friend. I would have made the lad something special. Please introduce me. Your mother is acting very mysterious about your little friend."

Poppy walked shyly out from behind Mom and over to me, looking intently at the old woman's face. He was dressed in a T-shirt, Levi's, his Redskins cap, and sneakers. His one stipulation in shopping, according to Aunt Ruth, was that all his clothes had to "be like Con's." And Aunt Ruth, who had longed for the day she could take her own son shopping, was happy enough to oblige. Except for a few scars on his chin and cheek and too-thin frame, he looked like any ordinary American kid.

"Mia . . ." I started to explain. But before I could say another word she gasped, her trembling hands shaking the metal walker as she collapsed into her chair.

"Oh my," she said over and over. "Oh my . . . oh my . . . oh my."

Mom rushed to her side and knelt down beside Mia's chair, patting her arm.

Somehow I knew that, from deep within the recesses of Mia Rozstoski's mind, a powerful memory had returned. She recognized the face of her friend Gabriel staring back at her through the eyes of a child.

"Mia." I brought Poppy by the hand, and together we squatted down so she could look into his face. "Hannah and I want you to meet our new friend. His full name is Gabriel Levi Goldberg. But you can call him Poppy. All his friends do."

"Gabriel," she whispered instead. She reached out and patted his hand and wept.

"It's the eyes. . . . They're so like Gabriel's," she finally managed.

I had never seen her cry in all the years I'd known her. Now tears streamed freely down her old face from happiness and wonder.

"He does belong to Gabriel, doesn't he?" she said in an unsteady voice, drying her tears with a starched white hand-kerchief. "Gabriel's grandson, I presume."

"You presume right," I said proudly.

"Welcome, Gabriel Levi Goldberg. Your grandfather was my dearest friend."

I thought she was going to let go the tears again—Mom and Hannah were sniffling away—but Frau R. had regained her regal composure, her emotions back in check.

Poppy sat down cross-legged on the Persian carpet, chin in hand. He looked up at her and said in Romanian, "Tell me about my grandfather."

For some time it was as though no one in that room existed but the two of them as the count's daughter explained to the abandoned child a story that they alone in the world shared. She told him about the Jewish man she hid on her estate and about their friendship, about his intelligence, kindness, faith, friendship, and how he gave his life to save her own.

Hannah, eyes glistening, gave me the I-told-you-she-was-in-love-with-him look.

The tea was forgotten. No one moved as Mia spoke. Poppy hung on every word. The Goldbergs had given him a future and a life when they adopted him; Frau Rozstoski was giving him back his past.

Afraid my own emotions might give way, I walked to the French doors, which were open to the balcony, and stood there gazing at the Donners' apartment while I listened to the now familiar tale.

What the locusts have eaten, God will restore. That was the phrase Gabriel had given to Mia on that fateful day. And now I understood. Through Poppy, Gabriel's family would go on, just as he hoped it would.

"Con, Hannah," Mia said, exhausted after telling her story, "now it is your turn. You must tell me how you *found* him. How has this wonderful thing happened?"

Hannah nodded at me, and I began, telling the tale as told to Ovi by Monica Popa, who when confronted with what we knew, told the rest.

"Andrei Popa read your inscription in the book, and it led him to Gabriel's widow, one of the Jews rounded up with all the others hiding out on the estate. It was probably much as we suspected. Rachel Levi faced a terrible choice: give her son to Monica and Andrei Popa in hopes of coming back for him, or take him with her to certain death on the train."

Mia's face was etched in pain. I stopped, but she waved her hand for me to go on.

"An eight-day-old baby had no chance on a transport train in January. I am sure Andrei told her that. So Rachel did the only thing she could, and Andrei and Monica, who had no children, raised him as their own."

"Are you all right, Mia?" Mom asked, sensing her distress.

"Yes, yes." She motioned Mom away. "Go on. . . . I must know."

"Mrs. Popa admitted that the baby's mother begged for one more night with her son," Hannah explained. "The next day when they returned, she gave him over to the enemy. The fact that he missed his bris saved his life."

I picked up the story again. "So the little Jewish boy became Popa. He was christened in the Orthodox Church, not because his new parents were religious, but because it gave them a piece of paper to show claim to the child. And no one ever knew—including Gabriel—that they were not his biological parents. It was such a dangerous, crazy time, and when the war was over, everyone wanted to forget as much as possible. Monica feared Rachel Levi would return, but of course, she didn't."

"In their own way they loved him," Hannah added. "Ovi was not able to get much out of her about how her son and daughter-in-law died—except that it was in a car accident, which Poppy either survived or wasn't involved in. Poppy was only a baby then, and she cared for him as long as she could. No money and poor health forced her to take him to the state orphanage, which was, as we explained, at Livada de Meri. Finally Monica Popa told Ovi that she would sign the papers so he could be adopted. And Uncle Aaron and Aunt Ruth took it from there. Matthew and Suzy Henry helped out, of course. I wish Con and I could have been there the day he got into their car and drove away, his first memory of riding in a car."

"Nigel has a nice car," Poppy added, finally on a topic he understood.

"A boy after my own heart." I tapped the bill of Poppy's cap.

One month after we saw her in the old folks home, Monica Popa died at the age of ninety. For Poppy's sake we kept that part of the story brief, and I went on to describe our picnic celebration with Poppy that nearly ended in disaster.

Frau Rozstoski was shocked at the news that Hans Grunwald had found us in Iasi, followed us to the grounds of Livada de Meri, and died trying to seek his revenge.

"Uncle Aaron and Mr. Szegedi recognized Grunwald in one of Hannah's pictures from the demonstration," I explained. "They of course realized we were in danger if he was in Iasi. Aunt Ruth *did* try to warn Hannah on the phone, but with the bad connection Hannah misunderstood her. When Ovi called a second time, as Hannah had asked him to do,

Uncle Aaron called the orphanage and spoke with Matthew Henry, who told him about the black car that had followed us there that Saturday. The ambassador rushed to Livada de Meri with Lazlo Szegedi, Andrew Hart, and a couple of marines, just in case. They arrived a bit too late to arrest Grunwald—disappointing Szegedi—but everyone seemed glad enough it wasn't me in the river."

"Thank God you are both safe," Mia said, shaking her head. "You do get into trouble, don't you, Con? Always did. You may not be my 'littlest angel' anymore, but a whole host of angels couldn't have made me as happy as I am today . . . thanks to you and Hannah."

She was struggling with her emotions but kept her chin set, her voice steady. "I am happier this moment than I have been since that day at Livada de Meri before Gabriel died. I remember thinking how glad I was to have something valuable to give him, something that might protect the life of his son. And you know what? I was right. It did in a way, didn't it?" She patted Poppy on the head and beamed.

"Yes, indeed. God works in mysterious ways," Mom said, standing up. "I'm exhausted from all this emotion. Let's have tea and celebrate. Mia has made your favorite cake, Con. Nigel, let's put the kettle on."

Hannah and I looked at each other over Poppy's head and agreed without words that Frau R. probably did need some tea before our next surprise.

"Poppy," Mia said, pulling herself up on the walker, "when Con was a little boy about your age, he liked very much my homemade chocolate ice cream. Would you like for me to make you some the next time you come to visit me?"

Poppy, who had tasted no sweets whatsoever for most of his life, wisely said, "Yes, please."

But he didn't seem to miss the chocolate ice cream as he happily tucked into the creamy Austrian Sachertorte Frau R. had made for tea and served on her best china. Sunshine streamed in through a high window behind Poppy, highlighting his thick black hair, perfectly cut.

After our celebration had been cleared away and more stories of Iasi had been told, we returned to the sitting room as the sun began to set in the western sky, slowly dropping behind the Alps.

"Poppy has a present for you," I said to Frau R., steadying her arm slightly as she once again sank down into her comfortable chair.

"Oh my, no," she protested, looking at the boy who had taken his place in front of her chair again. "Seeing Poppy is all the present I could ever want. I shall never need another."

"You get to explain." I poked Hannah. "If it hadn't been for you, I would have gone skiing and we wouldn't have this present for Frau R."

"No way, Con. You tell her."

"Please, one of you tell her," Mom said.

I took a deep breath and began. "Remember when we told you about finding the widow of Andrei Popa in the state home and how sick and miserable and totally poor she was . . . how she had stuffed all of her possessions in a dirty pillowcase under the bedcovers?" I paused.

"Yes, yes. I may be nearly a century old, but my memory is intact. Besides, I shall never forget one word of all you and Hannah have told me today. Proceed, please."

"Well, she gave us something from that bag hidden under her covers—something we almost threw away because it smelled so bad."

I nodded to Poppy, who had his hands behind his back.

He brought his hands around and laid a parcel wrapped in clean brown paper in Frau Rozstoski's lap.

The room grew very still. Only the ticking of the Viennese grandfather clock carried on.

Maria Rozstoski picked up a silver letter opener from the table beside her and slit the tape holding the wrapping paper.

"Oh no . . . it cannot be . . ." she stuttered, unable to take it in. Her shaking hands dropped the book into her lap.

"Thank you, Con. When I asked you, I never even dreamed . . . My father gave me . . . Oh dear, I can't quite take it in."

Hannah nudged me, and I knelt beside Mia's chair. I hugged her tight, picked up the book of Psalms, and fanned the fore edge, watching with her as the gilt disappeared. There she was, a girl again, back at Livada de Meri sitting in the shade under the spreading branches of the tall birch tree.

◆

"There is one last thing," I said to Frau Rozstoski as we got ready to go. "Hannah would like to take a photograph of you."

I knew what her response would be. She hated pictures and always refused.

"Please," I added before she could reply. "I think you owe me one."

Hannah took very special care to get this picture right.

EPILOGUE

IT WAS LATE AFTERNOON ON A LOVELY DAY IN MAY WHEN Rabbi Altar received his mail. Among the assorted envelopes was a letter postmarked from Vienna, Austria. Curious, he opened it at once.

The rabbi smiled as he read, remembering the two young people who had visited him in January. A photograph dropped out of the envelope onto his desk. He stared at the grand face for a long, long time. Then he put on his silk tallith and climbed the rickety stairs to his place of remembrance in the attic of the last synagogue in Iasi.

Rabbi Altar's hands shook as he removed one of the pictures from the wall. He sat down alone in the dusty room, surrounded by the memories of a time before the flames, and pried the cracked pane of glass out of the old wooden frame. Carefully, he rearranged the six dim photographs, making room for one more, this one sharp and clear. Then Rabbi Altar said a kaddish for Maria Rozstoski, "righteous gentile," who had loved mercy and acted justly as her God required.

AUTHOR'S NOTE

LIKE THE FIRST TWO BOOKS IN THE PASSPORT TO DAN-
ger trilogy, *Checkmate in the Carpathians* is a work of fiction
set in a historical context that includes some real characters
and events. The story takes place in the city of Iasi, which is
located on Romania's border with Moldova. Moldova is a
small, sovereign state that was carved out of the Ukraine after
the collapse of the Soviet Union.

King Carol was still on the throne of Romania at the beginning of World War II, but he soon assigned most of his
power to the prime minister, a fascist named Ion Antonescu,
who led the government and ran the country. Marshal Antonescu was the only leader in Europe besides Hitler who, with
the help of the brutal Iron Guard, planned his own full-
fledged killing operation.

Although the formal governmental role of the Iron Guard
ended in January 1941 through an internal political struggle,
the anti-Jewish spirit of the organization lived on in Antonescu's soldiers, who, like Hitler's SS, ruthlessly murdered Jewish Romanian citizens. So while the June 1941 murder of four
thousand Jews in Iasi was technically not committed by the
Iron Guard, for simplicity's sake, the Romanian soldiers under
Antonescu are referred to as the Iron Guard, here and
throughout the book.

Sadly, the unspeakable suffering of the Jewish people under Hitler was replicated in Romania, where tens of thousands of Jewish Romanians were removed from Iasi and other cities and villages and taken by freight train to the government's "mobile killing units." At the end of World War II, most of Romania's Jewish community—once the third largest in Europe—had been killed. To this day, there are fewer than one thousand Jews living in Iasi, a city of several hundred thousand.

In 1996, to pacify a small but militant voice of anti-Semitic sentiment in the population, the Romanian government built a monument to Ion Antonescu in Bucharest and invited the American diplomatic community to attend the unveiling ceremony. The American ambassador declined the invitation. For the purposes of the story, in *Checkmate in the Carpathians* the unveiling ceremony has been "moved" to Iasi and pushed ahead a few years.

The character of Frau Maria Rozstoski is based on the life of a real woman by the same name who was born in a castle on the banks of the Prut River, where she could see Ukrainian soldiers from her bedroom window. Twice, invading armies from Russia overran her family's estate. She was imprisoned by the Communists who took power at the end of World War II. Frau Rozstoski died at the age of ninety in the Austrian village of Grossgmain, where she was finally able to live in peace after her escape from Romania in 1970.

Again the shrewd reader may notice some geographic liberties taken in the name of fiction. The real Frau R.'s castle would have been situated close to the city of Czernowitz, now in the Ukraine but once part of the Austro-Hungarian Empire and, later, of Romania. In *Checkmate in the Carpathians* Livada de Meri is located in the fictional town of Barsa, on the Prut River, outside of Iasi. If Barsa existed it would indeed look across the river to a different country—Moldova, once part of the Soviet Union. But at the outbreak of World War I, in 1914, both sides of the Prut were in Romanian territory.

The people of Romania finally brought down Communism in 1989 in a bloody but successful uprising against Nicolae Ceausescu—one of Europe's most cruel dictators. The revolution began outside a small church in Timisoara on December 16 when faithful parishioners made a human barrier to protect their pastor from arrest by the Securitate, Ceausescu's fearsome secret police. Their brave stand for freedom spread to other cities. Thousands of people filled the streets, despite armored vehicles firing on them. They sang hymns and openly knelt in prayer after fifty years of being forced to worship in secret. Two weeks later, on Christmas Day, 1989, the repressive regime of Nicolae and Elena Ceausescu ended. But fifty years of Communism had left the country devastated. The fabric of the family, of community life, and of the economy had been systematically destroyed. Most of the population was reduced to living in badly built and impersonal high-rise buildings. And worst of all, over 150,000 abandoned children were left in orphanages like the one in this story.

One final note concerns the Odessa, the clandestine escape organization of the SS underground, which has helped many Nazi murderers, such as the character Herr Donner, elude justice. In the early 1950s Odessa was replaced by the Kameradenwerke ("Comrade Workshop"). The Kameradenwerke continued Odessa's work and expanded it to build an international network of supporters. For simplicity's sake, the movement's original name has been used throughout the PASSPORT TO DANGER series.

Young Adult Fiction Series From Bethany House Publishers

(Ages 12 and up)

CEDAR RIVER DAYDREAMS • by Judy Baer
Experience the challenges and excitement of high school life with Lexi Leighton and her friends.

GOLDEN FILLY SERIES • by Lauraine Snelling
Tricia Evanston races to become the first female jockey to win the sought-after Triple Crown.

JENNIE MCGRADY MYSTERIES • by Patricia Rushford
A contemporary Nancy Drew, Jennie McGrady's sleuthing talents bring back readers again and again.

LIVE! FROM BRENTWOOD HIGH • by Judy Baer
The staff of an action-packed teen-run news show explores the love, laughter, and tears of high school life.

PASSPORT TO DANGER • by Mary Reeves Bell
Constantine Rea, an American living in modern-day Austria, confronts the lasting horrors of the Holocaust.

THE SPECTRUM CHRONICLES • by Thomas Locke
Adventure awaits readers in this fantasy series set in another place and time.

SPRINGSONG BOOKS • by various authors
Compelling love stories and contemporary themes promise to capture the hearts of readers.

UNMISTAKABLY COOPER ELLIS • by Wendy Lee Nentwig
Laugh and cry with Cooper as she strives to balance modeling, faith, and life at her Manhattan high school.

WHITE DOVE ROMANCES • by Yvonne Lehman
Romance, suspense, and fast-paced action for teens committed to finding pure love.